I0684414

Turbo-Time Troopers

A Sci-Fi Epic

Joseph Melugin

Copyright ©2026 by Joseph Melugin

All rights reserved.

No part of this publication may be reproduced, distributed, or transmitted in any form or by any means, including photocopying, recording, or other electronic or mechanical methods, without the prior written permission of the publisher, except as permitted by U.S. copyright law. For permission requests, contact [include publisher/author contact info].

The story, all names, characters, and incidents portrayed in this production are fictitious. No identification with actual persons (living or deceased), places, buildings, and products is intended or should be inferred.

Book Cover by Joseph Melugin, with the assistance of AI.

1st edition 2026

Contents

To My Father David,
and My Grandfather Virgil.

Prologue

THE BETRAYAL OF
ULRAKK & THE FIRST KEY

"The Betrayal of UlRakk"

Before the first human dreamed of stars, the stars dreamed of us.

The chamber was not built but grown — coral metal rising in spirals, veins of living light pulsing through its walls. Within it, the air shimmered like a thought unfinished. Here, at the heart of the Amibian Throneworld, the High Convergence waited.

Six eyes opened in the darkness.

UlRakk of the Second Current stood before the living throne, four arms folded across a chest of pale, shifting flesh. His voice, when it came, was like the vibration of deep water.

"The experiment thrives, Great Lord. The humans have multiplied. They build, they learn, they reach for the heavens. They mirror us."

From the throne came no sound, only movement — a shape uncoiling from shadow. The god wore no single form; its edges were all wrong, always changing. Eyes bloomed and vanished. Mouths whispered geometry. Its presence filled the chamber like the pressure of a storm.

Nyarlathotep.

"They are failures, UlRakk," the god murmured, its words forming directly inside his mind. "A species without obedience. They climb, but not toward me. They create, yet they do not worship. They must be pruned."

The six eyes blinked in unison. "You made us gardeners, not butchers. They are still young."

"I am no gardener. I am continuity. They are noise."

Around them, other Amibian elders stood in silent orbit — their tendrils trembling, their colors dulled by fear. UlRakk saw resignation in their postures. They would obey. They always did.

But he could not.

"Lord of the Endless," UlRakk said carefully, "they carry our blood. They will surpass us in time. That is your gift."

Nyarlathotep's many mouths smiled in opposite directions.

"Then I will take back my gift."

It raised a hand — or something that resembled one — and from the floor rose two objects of unbearable beauty: one violet, one gold. They pulsed with power older than galaxies.

The god's voice rolled through the chamber like thunder underwater.

"The Keys of Continuum. One bends dimension. One bends time. Together they rewrite existence. With them, I will harvest every timeline at once. The humans will be undone before they were born."

UlRakk bowed low. Too low.

In that motion, his lower hands reached behind his back. One grasped a quantum seal, the other the hilt of a plasma blade. His upper hands trembled—not with fear, but decision.

He rose slowly. "Then forgive me, Lord. I will not serve the undoing of my children."

The strike was impossibly fast. The blade ignited with a scream of blue fire. He severed the energy conduits feeding the chamber before the god could reconfigure its shape. The floor convulsed; light bled out of the coral walls.

"You dare!!!" Nyarlathotep's voice tore through matter itself.

UlRakk seized the twin Keys, one in each hand. Their energies burned through his carapace, carving light where flesh once was. He turned toward the cosmic gate, already collapsing.

"I dare... for them!!."

The god's shadow lashed out, tearing one of UlRakk's arms from his body, but the Amibian hurled the violet Key into the breach. Space folded, screaming. A thousand reflections of reality shattered outward.

He hurled the gold Key after it, toward a second fracture on a distant axis.

Two Earths, two echoes — one for each Key.

Nyarlathotep's tendrils wrapped around him, crushing, unmaking.

"You cannot hide them from me, traitor. I am in all worlds."

UlRakk's six eyes dimmed, but he smiled — a rare human expression he had once copied from a scientist he'd watched through a telescope.

"Then... may you learn from them... what disobedience costs."

Light consumed the chamber.

When the glare faded, the Throneworld was silent.

Where UlRakk had stood, only ash drifted in zero gravity.

Far across the multiverse, two artifacts began to hum — each waiting for a pair of human hands.

And deep in the cosmic void, Nyarlathotep laughed — a sound like universes cracking.

The seeds had been scattered. The harvest had only begun.

"The First Key"

The sky had been bleeding for weeks.

LightBridge City—once the glittering crown of human progress—lay drowned in smoke and static. Towers that had scraped the stratosphere now burned like candles in a hurricane. The air reeked of ozone, ash, and grief. The war had ended, but nothing about the world said peace.

Victor Redmond walked through what was left of it, his boots crunching over glass and memory. Every ruined street whispered his failure. Every silence reminded him of them—Jay, whose laughter still haunted his ears, and their son, the boy who had wanted to build machines that healed instead of killed. Both gone in the final strike, vaporized in the name of a "better tomorrow."

He had fought for that tomorrow.

Now it looked like this.

Every radio frequency screamed white noise—except one. A whisper. A pulse.

Three quick beats, one long, two quick.

A pattern threading through the static like a heartbeat that refused to die.

He followed it down through the ruins.

The old subway grid was a tomb of steel and ice. Signs still flickered the names of places that no longer existed. At the bottom of the descent, behind a half-melted vault door, he found it—a chamber grown from living coral-metal, breathing faintly in the dark.

In its center hovered a shard of violet crystal, suspended in invisible threads of magnetism. The light from it refracted through dust, painting the wreckage in shifting hues of blue and red.

Victor stared for a long time. His reflection stared back—three mirrored versions of his face fractured across the crystal's facets. One young. One burning. One hollow.

"So this is what you left behind," he whispered. His voice shook with awe and rage.

The reflection moved half a second late and whispered back, "This is what you'll become."

He reached out. The shard met his palm.

The world screamed.

Fire and geometry. Oceans boiling. Stars crying out. A shape of impossible angles devouring galaxies.

And a voice—not heard, but felt through every nerve: Nyarlathotep.

I know your pain, it said within him.

Serve me, and you will never lose anything again.

Victor fell to his knees, laughter and sobs tearing from the same wound.

"Humanity is a curse," he gasped. "Endless war. Endless loss. Let it burn."

The violet light crawled up his arm, etching his veins into runes of living code. Flesh became data. Data became will. He felt his soul split open, and something vast stepped through.

Outside, the auroras froze mid-flicker.

The sky split, revealing a wound of white fire—a dimensional rift.

Victor rose, half man, half echo.

He didn't look back as he stepped into the scar.

Somewhere across another dimension, another LightBridge City slept in peace—unaware that its reflection had just crossed the veil to end it.

Chapter 1

IMPACT PATTERN

The train shouldn't have been that quiet.

Adam Warn watched the station's ads flutter against the glass as if the city's lungs had forgotten how to breathe. The lights dipped—three pulses, seventy-five milliseconds apart. He didn't time it. He felt it. A rhythm out of place.

He shifted his weight. The floor hummed back with a low, electrical heartbeat. The last time he'd felt that tone he'd been ten floors up, watching a conference-room window implode.

Then: white.

The blast swallowed sound. Air turned liquid. He was already moving, dragging a stranger with the copper scarf down behind a column. Shrapnel howled overhead. When silence finally broke free, it came in pieces—sirens, crying, the steady pop of broken fluorescents dying one by one.

Adam counted breaths. Five for him. Five for her. Five for the world. She was shaking but alive. He left her near an emergency exit and went the other way.

The secondary device was sloppy—wired for pressure, not timing. He disarmed it with a maintenance wand and geometry, not tools.

When the third charge coughed through the ceiling, the blast followed the vent shaft he'd given it, not the crowd.

When the dust settled, a new sound cut through: boots. Not police. Lighter. Balanced.

A woman stepped from the smoke in an ash-gray tactical coat. She moved like the chaos around her was choreography she already knew.

"Adam Warn," she said. "Walk with me."

He should have demanded to know who she was. Instead he fell in step beside her.

They reached the surface through a side corridor that smelled of wet concrete and ozone. Night had fallen while the world burned. Hover-drones swept beams of blue light across cratered pavement, scanning for life signs.

In the reflection of a shattered window, Adam saw himself haloed in siren light: soot-streaked, jacket torn, eyes too calm. The woman—Commander Reyes, her badge finally said—was talking into an earpiece, giving codes that made the drones back away.

"Casualties minimal considering the payload," she told someone unseen. "Our asset confirmed predictive pattern response. Recruit viable."

She turned back to him. "You have two choices, Mr. Warn. Go home and pretend you didn't just out-think a tri-layer Amibian mimic charge—or come with me and learn why that bomb existed in the first place."

"Amibian?" he asked. The word felt wrong in his mouth.

She opened a small case. Inside lay a fragment of black glass etched with shifting light. It looked alive. "Not human. Extraterrestrial. And very old. We've been reverse-engineering their tech since before you were born. Someone out there just weaponized it again."

"Who?"

"His name is Victor Redmond." Her gaze held his. "You're connected to him. We don't know why."

Something in his chest went cold. "Connected how?"

"That's classified," she said. "Until you sign in."

She closed the case and walked toward an armored transport idling by the curb. "If you want answers—and if you want Evelyn Lu back—you'll get in the truck."

The name hit harder than the explosion. "How do you—"

"Because he took her."

The city lights blurred for a second. He climbed in.

The transport roared skyward on silent repulsors. Through the narrow window, the city shrank into a lattice of firebreaks and emergency beacons.

Reyes watched a holo-feed of the blast site scrolling with spectral data. "We've been intercepting Redmond's dimensional signatures for weeks. Each one stronger than the last. He's using an artifact that folds reality sideways—a Dimensional Key. He's hunting for something else here: a companion device tied to time itself."

"And Evelyn?"

"Collateral. He's searching for a genetic marker—a match to someone he lost. You should understand, Mr. Warn: none of this is random."

Adam stared out the window. Patterns overlay the skyline—fault lines, heat signatures, mathematical symmetry in ruin. He didn't understand them. He just saw them.

"Why me?" he asked.

"Because you see what others miss. And because when things break, you run toward the fault."

The transport descended through clouds into a canyon of steel. A blast door irised open to reveal a hangar the size of a stadium. Rows of TurboFrames stood in docking clamps—sleek exo-suits black as oil, jointed like predatory insects, spines humming with blue energy. Mechanics in armored smocks moved between them, ghost-quick.

Reyes led him across the deck. "Project Turbo-Trooper. Earth's answer to an inter-dimensional war no one's supposed to know exists."

One of the suits swiveled its helmet toward him, optics flaring alive for a heartbeat, as if the machine were curious.

Reyes stopped beside a suit marked T-01 / RONIN. "This one's calibrated for you. Neural sync ninety-eight percent. We ran the scan while you were unconscious after Easton."

"I was never unconscious after—"

"You were," she said flatly. "For three minutes and twenty-six seconds. Long enough to read you. You've been on our list since then."

Adam ran his hand along the armor. The surface vibrated faintly, like it was breathing under his palm.

"You'll start training tomorrow," Reyes said. "But first, there's someone you should meet."

Glass walls. Floating data streams. The air smelled faintly of ozone and disinfectant. A hologram rotated above the table—a three-dimensional model of a cyborg man's face, eyes closed as if in sleep.

Victor Redmond.

"Intelligence confirms he's operating under another name in several dimensions," said Reyes. "He leads Amibian forces and answers to something... ancient. A being we code-name Nyarlathotep."

The hologram flickered; behind Redmond's features a shadow moved, too many angles to be human.

Reyes killed the feed. "We don't know its goal yet, only that it wants both artifacts joined. If that happens, every timeline collapses into one—his."

She tossed him a small badge etched with the Turbo-Trooper insignia: a wing bisected by a spiral. "Welcome to the line between worlds, Captain Warn."

He caught it without looking. His reflection in the table looked older than he remembered.

Outside the glass, lightning crawled across the clouds, painting the hangar in brief stutters of light. The pattern—three flashes, one pause, two more—was identical to the flicker before the explosion.

Adam stared at it until the rhythm carved itself into his mind. He didn't know why yet. Only that it mattered.

The transport punched through a curtain of stormcloud and into darkness so complete it looked carved. A moment later, the night itself split—ice cliffs rearing on either side like the teeth of a world-sized predator.

"South Pole sector, classified grid E-9," Reyes said. "Officially, this region doesn't exist."

Below them a gulf of frozen ocean opened, rimmed by walls of blue ice hundreds of meters tall. The pilots angled downward toward what looked like solid glacier. At the last instant, the ice fractured along geometric seams and folded away, revealing a shaft lit from within by rows of amber lights. The craft descended into the glow and the Arctic storm closed overhead, erasing all trace.

"Welcome to Outpost Heian-Ridge," Reyes said. "Joint command—Japanese Defense Agency and U.S. Strategic Science Division. The press calls it Project Amaterasu when they whisper. We call it home."

The bay stretched for kilometers under the ice, a cathedral of machinery. American flags and red-sun crests hung side by side between cooling towers. Steam rose in white ribbons from coolant vents. Rows of Turbo-Trooper suits—sleek black armor sculpted with samurai-sharp contours—stood in power racks humming like distant thunder.

Technicians in mixed uniforms moved in practiced silence. Some wore the angular badges of DOCSW, others the kanji for Kōkaku Sentōbu, the Japanese cyber-combat branch. Their voices—English and Japanese, code words and quick data—braided into one language of war.

"This is where the first TurboFrames were born," Reyes said. "American brawn, Japanese precision. The suits fuse quantum-fiber musculature with neural relay matrices. You don't pilot them—you become them."

She handed him a tablet. Data scrolled in blue firelight: T-01 / RONIN — Neural Sync 98.6%.

"Why Antarctica?" Adam asked.

"Two reasons," Reyes said. "Isolation... and history. When the Amibian artifacts were unearthed in the forties, they pulsed only near magnetic true south. We built over that pulse."

They crossed a bridge above a reactor pit where molten light churned like bottled sunrise. The heat fogged Adam's visor; when it cleared, he saw a mural painted on the far wall—an ancient creature, half-squid, half-man, surrounded by stars and chains.

Inside the command balcony, Reyes poured two cups of bitter synth-coffee. She handed him one and leaned against the rail.

"Let's set expectations," she said. "I'm your CO, but my real job is simpler—I get you ready before this war eats you. You'll learn faster than the others, but you'll crash harder too. I've seen it before."

"Why me, really?" Adam asked.

"Because the patterns talk to you. That's not training—that's wiring. Don't waste it."

Her tone softened for the first time. "You'll hear rumors that the Troopers are ghosts—soldiers pulled from timelines that no longer exist. Don't let the myths get in your head. Stay grounded, Warn. Remember who you are before you start asking what you are."

Later, in the briefing dome, holographic constellations swirled overhead as Reyes activated an archive. The lights dimmed; alien silhouettes spun into being.

"The Amibian," she said. "Old as oceans. They called themselves the First Current. Six-eyed, four-armed, walking humanoid squids standing two meters tall. Their smallest caste—the Pawns—can flip an armored car. The Knights can throw one, and that is a fraction of the soldier types"

Adam watched their digital muscles ripple like liquid.

"They seeded humanity," Reyes continued. "Across thousands of worlds and dimensions. Grew us like crops to test evolution's limits. Most Amibian saw us as property. But one of their council—Ul-Rakk—sided with us when the cosmic entity Nyarlathotep claimed their empire. UlRakk stole two artifacts the god coveted: the Dimensional Key and the Chronal Key. He scattered them to separate Earths so Nyarlathotep couldn't fuse time and reality into one leash."

"Victor found the Dimensional Key in his world," she said. "Yours holds the other. That's why you're both here—why the universe itself seems to pivot around you."

The hologram shifted to show twin orbs: one pulsing violet, one gold. Between them, a filament of energy—cut, trembling, incomplete.

"UlRakk bought humanity a few thousand years," Reyes said quietly. "Nyarlathotep wants that debt paid."

The briefing dome opened onto an observation deck facing the ice wall. Beyond the transparent barrier, auroras coiled through the polar night in silent ribbons of green and crimson. Somewhere beneath that light, the Amibian pulse hummed through the planet's bones.

Reyes stood beside him. "Out there is everything we're trying to keep breathing. The line between worlds runs through this base. You'll help me hold it."

Adam looked down at the badge still warm in his hand—Turbo-Trooper wings split by a spiral—and felt the pattern settle into memory.

He didn't know if he was ready.

But he knew the rhythm of the lights overhead—three quick, one long, two quick.

And rhythms meant messages.

Whatever awaited beyond that ice wall, he would learn to read it.

Chapter 2

SUIT UP

Morning inside Outpost Heian-Ridge didn't begin with sunrise.

It began with sound—a low vibration running through the floors, the reactors, the bones of every soldier who lived beneath the ice.

Adam Warn woke to that hum. It reminded him of a heartbeat inside metal.

"On your feet, recruits! You sleep, you die!"

The voice that shattered the quiet belonged to Sergeant John Wolfgrove, a man carved out of old wars and bad coffee. He was a walking direct order, his jaw dusted with iron-gray stubble. He wore no exo-suit, only a thick jacket that looked bulletproof by attitude alone.

Three soldiers stood before him on the training deck:

Adam Warn, call sign Ronin (T1).

Dexter Yoi, call sign Samurai (T2).

Jose Fuentes, call sign Ninja (T3).

"Troopers," Wolfgrove barked, pacing between them, "you are not tanks. You are scalpels. You are ghosts. You are humanity's last argument before extinction. Move like it."

Dex grinned. "Permission to crack a joke, sir?"

"Denied, Yoi."

"Already did, sir."

Jose smirked despite himself. Adam just sighed in Annoyance.

Rows of armor stood in the hangar like sentinels waiting for souls. Sleek black frameworks of alloy and biotech muscle, spines pulsing with blue light. Each bore its class sigil:

T1 / RONIN — assault, speed, agility.

T2 / SAMURAI — precision, long-range, technical systems.

T3 / NINJA — infiltration, stealth, subversion.

No heavy armor. No tanks. Turbo-Troopers fought fast or died faster.

Technicians moved between the racks, slotting neural cables and sidearms: assault rifles, shotguns, pistols, submachine guns, sniper systems.

Technicians loaded neural links, ran diagnostics, and fitted weapons: rifles, pistols, shotguns, sub-machine guns, sniper systems. Every trooper carried a mono-blade, a sword forged from Amibian resonance steel—alive with faint vibrations. When all else failed, steel still told the truth.

Wolfgrove stalked down the line, cigar unlit between his teeth.

Wolfgrove's voice carried over the hum.

"Today, you learn the TURBO Function. It's the difference between victory and vaporization."

He tapped the back of Adam's neck where a small neural disk pulsed beneath the skin.

"TURBO heightens your senses, slows your world, and silences your pain. You'll move through explosions like smoke." He paused, eyes narrowing. "But it comes with a cost. The longer you stay in it, the closer your brain gets to cooking itself. Don't stay in TURBO to be a hero. Use it to live."

Dex muttered, "Adrenaline with a kill switch. Nice."

Wolfgrove's glare could have stopped a missile. "Yoi, when you're a corpse, try not to waste my oxygen.

After the physical drills came silence.

The troopers entered a chamber lit by soft white panels. No equipment. No noise. Just stillness.

Commander Reyes waited at the front, hands clasped behind her back.

"This next phase isn't about your body," she said. "It's about your mind. We call it The Chair."

Dex looked around. "There's no chair, ma'am."

Reyes smiled. "Exactly. It's in your head."

She paced slowly, voice level and deliberate.

"The Chair is an Amibian discipline—psychological warfare training. When their soldiers faced terror, they visualized themselves in an unbreakable chair. They didn't fight fear. They sat in it. Unmoved. The Chair became a mental anchor in the storm."

Wolfgrove folded his arms. "You learn it now, or you die screaming later."

Reyes's tone softened. "Close your eyes. Picture it. The shape, the material. Whatever keeps you steady. Then, when your mind starts to fracture, sit. Don't run. Don't fight. Endure."

Adam's eyes closed.

In his mind, he saw it instantly—a chair of brushed steel floating in white silence.

No shadows. No walls. Only sound: a low pulse matching his heartbeat.

Whispers crept in—Evelyn's voice, the blast from the station, the static that had haunted him since childhood. He traced the rhythm beneath it, found the pattern, and let the noise fade around him.

He sat.

When he opened his eyes, the room was still. Reyes nodded. "That's how you survive."

Dex groaned. "Mine was on fire."

Jose shrugged. "Mine broke in half."

"Both alive," Reyes said. "That counts."

Wolfgrove's stare lingered on Adam. "You didn't flinch. Remember that."

Later that night, Dex and Jose cornered him in the mess hall, trays forgotten.

"You hear the rumor?" Dex asked, half-grinning. "About the Amibian tech Victor Redmond's been spreading? Tiny bio-mechs—Tech-Mites. They latch onto the neural ports of Tur-boFrames and rewrite command signals. Turn soldiers into puppets."

"Sounds like a ghost story," Jose muttered.

"Or a bad one," Dex said. "The kind that ends with us shooting our own."

Adam didn't speak. The image of the Chair still burned in his mind—those whispering voices, something cold threading through them that didn't feel entirely human.

He wondered, just for a heartbeat, if the Tech-Mites were already real.

If the Amibian hadn't built the Chair to protect minds—but to test which ones could be broken.

Days bled together.

Dex became the laughter that filled the silences; Jose, the calm that held them steady; Adam, the force that kept them moving forward.

They sparred, sweated, bled, learned.

They joked, they drank and played pool in the barracks, argued about music, made bets on Wolfgrove's kill count.

When one of them fell, the others lifted him.

When one of them faltered, the others shouted him back to his feet.

Under the ice, friendship became armor.

Wolfgrove called them nickname of "The Unbreakables".

Reyes said nothing, but her eyes carried pride—and something heavier, as if she could already see how this story might end.

Chapter 3

BAPTIZED BY FIRE

Above Earth, the Obsidian Ark drifted through the upper thermosphere, half machine, half cathedral.

From its observation deck, Victor Redmond watched lightning crawl across the planet's night side.

"Show him something to lose," he whispered.

A stasis pod hissed open behind him. Evelyn Lu gasped for air. Victor crouched beside her, chrome fingers brushing her hair.

"You're going home," he said. "Tell Adam Warn I remember."

Light fractured; reality bent. She vanished in a violet flare.

Victor rose. "Phase One complete. Begin the invasion."

In New Helios, a spire-city rising from the Atlantic shallows, dawn broke to the sound of orbital sirens.

Children pressed against apartment glass, pointing at the silver streaks descending through the clouds—until the first one hit.

Buildings folded inward. Air became fire. The ocean itself boiled where an Amibian carrier impacted the bay.

Within minutes, the city's population of nine million screamed in unison. The sound became weather.

Inside the drop-ship, alarms bled red across the cabin.

"World's under siege!" Wolfgrove barked. "Move like you mean it!"

Adam sealed his Ronin frame. Dex checked his sniper systems; Jose whispered a prayer in Spanish that ended with a grin.

Commander Reyes met their eyes. "Primary objective: defend the artifact vault beneath Central Helios. Secondary: stay alive."

Dex: "Tertiary objective: impress the locals?"

Reyes: "They're all dead, Yoi."

The doors blew open. The planet screamed.

They jumped.

TURBO Function engaged.

Time fractured.

Adam fell through a storm of glass and plasma, every droplet hanging like crystal.

He hit the street, rifle roaring, rounds stitching through the chitin of an Amibian Pawn.

Its six eyes burst like bulbs; the carcass spasmed and collapsed across a car still full of civilians.

A woman inside pounded the windshield, mouth open, skin peeling from the heat.

Adam tore the door free, dragged her out, handed her to medics already dying.

Above them, a Knight—eight feet of muscle and light—ripped a gunner from his tank and split him in half like paper.

Jose's sword flashed once; the creature fell headless into the wreckage.

Dex's sniper round followed, punching through another's skull three blocks away.

"Target down," Dex said. "Two million to go."

A scream tore through comms—civilians trampled in evacuation tunnels, mothers smothering children to keep them quiet as drones passed overhead.

The air tasted of blood and iron filings.

Through the chaos, Adam saw movement—a civilian staggering through smoke.

Evelyn.

He ran.

She collapsed into his arms, ash clinging to her skin. "Adam... is it you?"

He nodded. "You're safe now."

Behind them, a hospital tower imploded, sending glass through the rain like daggers.

He shielded her with his frame, his voice steadier than it had ever been.

"I'm not losing you again."

Across the world, the invasion spread like infection.

Cairo drowned in plasma storms. Osaka vanished under an alien monsoon.

In Paris, soldiers fired into the sky until their rifles melted.

New Helios became the first wound of the new war.

Victor watched from orbit, his voice low. "Let them remember what it means to look up and pray."

They pray to me now, Nyarlathotep whispered.

Victor smiled. "Then let them worship."

By nightfall, the city was a furnace.

Bodies floated in flooded streets, light from burning towers reflecting in their glassy eyes.

Children sat beside parents who would never move again.

Soldiers dragged corpses into heaps and called them barricades.

The Turbo-Troopers fought through it all.

Adam moved like a weapon made of guilt.

Dex's laughter turned brittle over comms.

Jose killed in silence.

Reyes's voice crackled through static: "Team Sigma—sector north. Raptor-squad—hold sector twelve."

A plasma beam carved the sky.

Her signal vanished mid-word.

Dex froze. "No—no, that's not funny Reyes come on!"

"Move!" Adam shouted.

They pressed on through hell.

At midnight the horizon was liquid fire.

Every building was a pyre.

The surviving humans—soldiers, medics, children—moved like shadows through ash.

At the vault entrance, Adam, Dex, and Jose made their final stand.

Amibian Knights poured from the smoke; the trio fought like a single heartbeat.

When it was done, they stood knee-deep in alien corpses covered in their blood.

The artifact—safe, for now.

The city—dead.

Wolfgrove's voice cracked over comms. "All surviving units, fall back. artifact is secured, enemy retreating."

Adam looked at the firestorm where Reyes had died. "at least we made sure she left when we had victory....."

Chapter 4

ASHES OF NEW HELIOS

The transport bay stank of scorched metal and fear. Bodies wrapped in polymer lined the hangar wall—names fading on their tags as condensation blurred the ink.

Wolfgrove stood beside the flag-draped form of Commander Reyes. No speech, only silence. The kind that weighed more than words ever could.

Dex broke it first. "She told me to shut up more." He forced a laugh that didn't last. "Guess she got the last word."

Jose exhaled through his nose. "She saved half the city."

"Half of nothing's still nothing," Dex muttered, rubbing the back of his neck.

Adam stood a step apart, helmet under one arm. The light from the hangar doors caught the burn marks on his armor. When he finally spoke, his voice was quiet enough that they leaned closer to hear.

"My dad used to say the same thing," Adam said. "That silence was the loudest kind of respect."

Dex frowned. "You never talk about him."

Adam nodded slowly. "He died during the Great Unity protests. He wasn't a soldier—just a man who believed people should have a choice in who runs their lives. I was home, doing homework, when it came on the newsfeed. He was standing in a crowd with a sign that said *'We are one, not owned.'* Then the shooting started."

He let the words settle. The hum of generators filled the pause.

Jose looked down. "That's rough, man."

"It was," Adam said, "but that's not the part I remember most." He smiled, small but real. "I remember him helping me fix a broken model jet. He said every machine has a pattern, you just have to listen for it. He taught me to hear things other people miss."

Dex nodded. "Sounds like the guy who made you... you."

"Yeah." Adam's gaze drifted toward Reyes's shrouded body. "When he died, I thought the good parts would die too. But they don't. They stay. You just have to keep them clean."

Jose clasped his shoulder. "Then we keep them clean together."

Dex added softly, "For her, too."

They stood there, three soldiers beneath the humming lights, each carrying ghosts that felt a little lighter because they were shared.

Across the bay, Wolfgrove finally spoke. "Rest easy, Commander. The living have work."

The hangar lights dimmed to half power. Outside the base walls, Antarctica howled—a lonely, endless wind that sounded almost like grief finding its voice.

The bodies were gone now, sealed and sent to the incineration chambers. Only the smell of fuel and burned cloth remained.

Dex and Jose sat near the bulkhead, polishing their weapons out of habit more than need. The silence between them was heavy, but not hostile—just tired.

Evelyn stood a few meters away, staring through the blast doors at the ice horizon. Her reflection trembled against the glass, pale and still.

Adam walked over quietly. "You should rest," he said.

She didn't turn. "I tried. Every time I close my eyes, I see the city again."

He nodded. "Me too."

She finally looked at him. "How do you deal with it? All this?"

Adam hesitated. Then: "You don't deal with it. You carry it, piece by piece, until it's not heavy anymore. My dad used to say pain's like fire—if you try to smother it, it spreads. But if you hold it steady, it becomes light."

Evelyn's eyes softened. "He sounds like someone who saw more than most."

"He did," Adam said. "He believed in people, even when they didn't deserve it. He used to fix old drones just so kids in the neighborhood could fly them. Said it reminded him what progress was supposed to mean."

He smiled faintly. "He died doing what he believed in. That doesn't make it okay—but it makes it worth remembering."

Evelyn stepped closer. "And Reyes?"

Adam looked down, his voice low. "She believed the same thing. Maybe that's why I followed her."

For a while they just stood there, the hum of the base filling the spaces their words couldn't.

Dex called from across the hangar. "Hey, lovebirds, if you two are done soul-searching, Jose's trying to teach me how to reload with one hand."

Jose didn't look up. "You'll blow the other one off."

Adam chuckled under his breath. For a second, the sound felt almost normal.

Evelyn smiled, faint but real. "They're good for you."

"Yeah," he said. "They are."

He looked back out at the frozen horizon—the reflection of himself, the memory of his father, the ghost of Reyes. "Tomorrow's not going to wait for us," he said quietly. "So we make sure it's worth waking up to."

Evelyn rested a hand on his arm. "Then wake up fighting."

The overhead lights flickered—three long, two short, one slow. Adam noticed, as always. He didn't know if it was just power fluctuation or something else watching through the circuits. But he smiled anyway, the kind of smile that dared the darkness to try again. He gave Evelyn a kiss before going back.

Chapter 5

THE ARK IN SHADOW

The base slept like a buried animal. Tunnels breathed recycled air. Red status LEDs blinked in rows like low, patient eyes. Somewhere far above the reinforced ice and granite, the Antarctic wind screamed over black rock and white desert, but down here—down where secrets lived—the sound was a deep, steady hum, like a mother ship idling.

Adam signed out of Medical under a light that flickered in a three-long, two-short cadence. He tried not to notice. Dex and Jose flanked him—one with a sling and a grin, the other with a quiet that could stop a room.

"Come on," Dex said, guiding him down a service corridor that smelled like coolant and citrus disinfectant. "You need an antiviral shot. It's called whiskey."

Jose keyed a door disguised as a maintenance locker. It thunked open on the Break Line—a narrow nook hacked into old storage: low ceiling, warped steel counter, three mismatched stools, a strip of fake neon in the shape of a lightning bolt. A sign hand-painted on a tool case read: IF YOU'RE READING THIS, YOU'RE OFF DUTY.

They took the stools. Dex reached under the counter and produced a battered bottle with a cracked label: Blackstar Synthe-Reserve. He poured three shots into ceramic mugs because glass shattered too easily on military floors.

They drank. It hit like a soft explosion, heat blooming through iron-cold blood.

Dex hissed. "Still tastes like someone carbonated a campfire." He set his cup down, squinted at Adam. "You with me, Ronin?"

Adam rolled the liquor on his tongue. "I'm here."

"Define 'here.'" Dex tapped Adam's temple with a finger. "Because your eyes are doing the haunted-lighthouse thing again."

"Leave him," Jose said gently, his own cup untouched. "We lost people."

The word hung there with the smoke-thin air. People: Reyes. Civilians in the corridors of New Helios. Nameless soldiers who bled for three more minutes of radio time. People.

Dex reached for the bottle again, then didn't. "We all got ghosts. Mine just swear at me in Spanish and tell me to sleep. I don't listen."

Adam watched the neon bolt flutter. In its failing light he saw a hundred reflections—train windows in a winter night, a flashing subway ad, the polished aluminum of a sink that never stayed clean. He drank again.

"I used to be a dishwasher," he said.

Dex blinked. "I thought you were going to say assassin or prodigy. You just... drop a dishwasher on me?"

"Just a kid," Adam said, "doing exactly what he was supposed to. Stack plates, scrape burned cheese off metal, spin-cut limes for water glasses nobody drank. I wore a plastic apron that smelled like lemons and yeast, and I figured if I kept my head down, I could be left alone. Not a soldier. Not a hero. Just the guy who kept the pipes from clogging."

Jose's eyes lifted. "When did that change?"

"The night the train crashed."

The hum of the base pressed closer, as if it, too, leaned in to listen.

"Overpass on the east line," Adam said. "Freak frost storm. I was riding home after closing. Inventory in my backpack. My hands smelled like bleach and dishwater. I was watching the city blur—billboards, faces, lights in apartments where people were living lives—and I was counting. I always count. How many poles pass each second, how fast the ads flick, three long, two short, one pause." He smiled without warmth. "Then the world stuttered."

"Brakes?" Dex asked.

"Metal on metal. Sparks like meteors. We collapsed into the next car like someone tipped the world. I remember the sound of a child crying and thinking: don't panic, there's a pattern to this. I crawled. Pulled people loose. Used a tray from the café car as a lever. The train was twisting like a knife, and I kept hearing a rhythm I couldn't place and—" He stopped, swallowed. "—and when we broke the window, night air hit us and it smelled like the ocean, even in the city. I remember that. Salt and electricity."

Jose's voice was soft. "You saved people."

Adam looked down at the mug. "Some. Not all." A breath. "Some nights, I hear the ones I didn't."

Dex's hand landed on his shoulder. No jokes. No patter. Just weight. "We get through by bailing the boat we're in. Not the whole ocean."

Adam nodded once. "That night, they pulled me out last. If I did not go with Reyes I knew the EMT would've looked at me like I'd done something I didn't understand. The News would called me a 'good Samaritan' until they got bored and moved on. I would have gone back to work the next day, but something was wrong. The sink was too shallow. The night too quiet. Evelyn went missing the night before, and I had to bare watching the news again." He met their eyes. "Normal people would look for their Girlfriend after they went missing, I would feel uncapable as always, because I know with the world it all comes down to It's about what you are, not who you are. The uniform, the rank, the armor—it's paint. What you do when it breaks? That's the truth."

Jose finally lifted his cup and drank. He didn't flinch. "That's why Reyes liked you, for once reverse that saying, and see how your whole world changes."

Dex nodded toward the ceiling, toward the ice and sky beyond it. "The old woman's probably up there arguing with saints about perimeter discipline."

Silence again, but not empty this time. The three sat with it until the ache settled into something they could carry.

A chime buzzed—a soft priority ping from the corridor. Not an alarm. A summons.

Dex groaned. "Ten minutes of therapy and Command wants us wise again."

Jose stood, straightened his jacket with his good hand. "We're never wise. Just willing."

Adam capped the bottle, wiped the counter with a bar rag out of habit, and left the mug where it was—still wet, like a promise.

They stepped back into the corridor's pale light. Soldiers drifted past with eyes like scraped bone. A pair of techs wheeled a crate of replacement microturbines. Someone laughed too loudly, stopped, and apologized to no one. The war didn't end in bangs. It ebbed like a tide, and the things it left behind crawled.

The command amphitheater sat like a swallowed stadium—tiered rows, wrapped screens, a table at the bottom where power gathered. General Osei stood with both hands on the console, her posture saying fatigue, her eyes refusing it. Behind her, a three-dimensional projection of Earth turned under veils of static. LightBridge City looked like a scab.

"Raptor Squad," Osei said, voice steady. "At ease. We have a window before the next storm."

Dex leaned into Adam, whispered, "I hate windows. Everything bad fits through them."

Osei gestured and the projection snapped to a high-contrast render of the Moon—a crescent of ash and shadow. Across its dark side, a wound glowed: an array of hexagonal structures, each hive pulsing with cold light.

"This," Osei said, "is not a mine. Nor a base in the way we use the word. It is... a shipbuilding womb." A second image rolled: filaments like roots, drilling into regolith, threading something enormous under the surface. "Our deep-spectrum picked it up when the Ark's residue spiked. We believe the Amibian are gestating a vessel. Something bigger than what we've seen."

Dex lifted a hand without waiting to be called on. "Define 'bigger.' Like bigger than a destroyer? Or bigger than my regrets?"

"Capital-class," Osei said. "Maybe more. We don't know its limits. The object broadcasts on frequencies we can't map."

Jose's jaw tightened. "Orders?"

"Recon first. Surgical sabotage if we can manage it. We're assigning Raptor Squad to spearhead, because you've already broken their teeth twice this week." She glanced at Adam. "And because you don't stop."

Adam kept his face neutral. Inside, something unfolded—fear and relief in the same breath, the simple blessing of direction. Go. A word his bones understood.

"Any questions?" Osei asked.

"Yes," Dex said. "Do we get hazard pay or do we just eat more packets labeled 'beef' that taste like sadness?"

A faint smile ghosted Osei's mouth. "I'll see what Logistics can unearth in the ancient tomb that is our pantry." The smile died. "There's one more piece."

The display cut to Lab Seven—a sealed sublevel lit the color of pale water. Through the window: Evelyn. Dark hair tied back. Shadows under her eyes like painted wings. She wore a lab jacket over a service tee that didn't fit and a bracelet of hospital tags she hadn't yet cut off. She was alone at a console, hands moving, eyes scanning strings of language that weren't language.

"She came back," Dex murmured, surprise and relief leaking into his voice.

"She asked to help," Osei said. "She knows the architecture of their code by feel. I don't know if that's a blessing or a burn. Either way, it's ours to use."

Adam's mouth was dry. "Does she—"

"She's not a soldier," Osei said, in case someone in the room needed to hear that. "She stays here. You go there. Try not to die in the same hour."

The briefing dissolved into assignments and transport windows and code names that sounded like knives. Adam waited until the room thinned. When he moved toward the exit, Jose didn't follow, and Dex pretended not to notice, bundling his sling like it suddenly needed maintenance.

The corridor to Lab Seven ran colder. Security doors recognized Adam's biometrics and rolled open with soft hydraulic sighs. He wiped his palms on his pants—habit, not sweat—and stepped inside.

Evelyn didn't look up at first. The screens reflected in her eyes: graphs, waveforms, something that fell between heartbeat and tectonic shift. The room hummed with a frequency that made the hair on Adam's forearms lift.

She turned, and the world narrowed.

"Hey," she said, voice thinner than he remembered. She tried to smile and made it halfway. "You look worse."

"I've been told whiskey helps." He realized hands belonged somewhere and settled for hooking his thumbs in his belt. "You working with Osei now?"

"I'm working against..." Her gaze flicked to the speakers, as if the walls could listen. "Against it."

He nodded once. "Thank you."

"I'm not doing it for you," she said, too quickly, then softened, tired. "Not only for you."

They stood in the wash of the monitors' glow. Up close he could see the small scar at the base of her skull where the medics had cut; he didn't let his eyes linger.

"I used to be a dishwasher," he heard himself say, surprised by it the way someone is surprised a song has followed them from childhood. "I forget that when I'm in armor."

She studied him. "You think I only see the suit?"

"I'm saying the world keeps asking what we are. Rank. Unit. Asset." He shrugged. "I think it's about who."

Evelyn's mouth tightened, almost a smile, almost grief. "Who are you, Adam?"

"I'm a man who counts things he can't stop and jumps into fires he can't win." He took a slow breath. "And a man who would do it again if it meant one person lived."

Silence. The hum. On the screen, a waveform spiked, then steadied—like a heartbeat finding itself.

Her gaze slid past him to the glass, to the dim reflection of both of them standing in blue light. "I hear... patterns sometimes. Like words without vowels. It's probably nothing."

"It's probably something," he said. "It always is."

For a moment, the lab felt like a shelter: four walls, a light, a person who understood enough not to ask for more than was possible. Then the intercom clicked.

"Raptor Squad—armory in ten," Osei's voice said, clear as a blade.

Evelyn's hands went back to the keys. "Go save the world so I can finish saving the math."

Adam turned for the door, paused. "If I don't come back, tell Dex my last words were that he owes me fifty credits."

Her smile landed this time, a small sun. "Come back and tell him yourself."

He stepped into the corridor and let the door seal between them. The hum shifted again—three long, two short, one pause. He didn't flinch. He counted it. Owned it. Turned it into a march.

At the armory, Dex was giving the quartermaster grief about the pistol grips again and Jose was checking blade edges with a reverence he never gave to prayers. They looked up when Adam walked in, and for a second the three of them were just men in a room, not an answer to a question the universe shouldn't have asked.

"Tomorrow's mistake," Dex said, lifting an imaginary glass.

"Tomorrow's purpose," Jose countered.

Adam fit the sword to the magnetic clamp at his hip, racked his rifle, and felt the pieces of himself lock where they needed to be.

"Let's go see what's hiding on the dark side," he said.

Above them, beyond the stone and ice and screaming wind, the Moon waited. In its shadow, something impossibly old was learning to breathe.

The Moon hung over Earth like a half-closed eye. From orbit, its dark side gleamed with faint hexagonal scars—each one pulsing like a heartbeat beneath the surface. Inside the metallic labyrinth of the Obsidian Ark, Victor Redmond stood at a transparent viewport, his reflection a patchwork of man and machine.

Half of his face remained human, pale under the glow of alien circuitry. The other half shimmered in layers of silver filaments that moved when he breathed, like living veins of mercury. The stars outside flickered in synchrony with his artificial pulse.

Behind him, the Amibian overseers glided across the floor. Their six eyes blinked in perfect coordination, their tendrils brushing the air with whisper-like motions. They carried data tablets that pulsed with deep violet glyphs—languages only Nyarlathotep's servants could read.

"You're late," Victor said, his voice part static, part soul.

One of the creatures bent its legs into a respectful crouch. "The arrays are ready, my lord. The beam will reach your Earth's satellites within the next orbit."

Victor didn't turn. "And humanity will go deaf."

A ripple of laughter bled through the shadows—low, cosmic, wrong. Nyarlathotep didn't need a body. He was the tremor in the floor, the hiss in the cables, the whisper in Victor's skull.

"You speak as though they ever listened."

Victor's hand flexed, mechanical fingers scraping across the glass. "They will. One way or another."

"Do you still dream of her?"

His jaw clenched. "Dreams are human."

"And yet you keep one."

The glass fogged with his breath. In its reflection, for a split second, he didn't see a cyborg general. He saw a man in a train window. Hands clean, ring on his finger, laughter beside him. Jay.

He blinked, and she was gone. The machinery in his spine thrummed louder, purging sentiment with static.

"Activate the pulse," Victor ordered. "End the illusion."

Outside, the Ark's hexagonal panels began to spin, each turning like a clock gear until a massive lattice formed. Energy flared through its core—a column of darkness that swallowed light itself.

Raptor Base — Deployment Bay

The shuttle bay reeked of coolant, ozone, and old fear. Engineers rushed around the Raptor Squad's dropship, Falcon's Spear, tightening seals and checking pressure lines. The hum of fusion engines was a heartbeat under steel.

Adam stood in full armor, helmet locked under his arm. His mind replayed Evelyn's voice in the lab—soft, weary, strong.

Dex walked past, chewing a protein bar that looked like compressed dirt. "Last meal before the Moon. Think it's real beef?"

Jose grinned faintly. "If it moos, it's a lie."

Dex chuckled, but his humor was thinner than usual. "You think the Amibian even sleep?"

Adam glanced at him. "They dream of order. That's what makes them dangerous."

Dex shrugged. "I dream of beaches. Guess that makes me safe."

The overhead speakers barked, "Raptor Squad, launch in ten."

Osei's voice followed: "Mission parameters are simple. Get in. Confirm the Ark's location. Sabotage if possible. Return alive if the universe feels generous."

Dex leaned against the bulkhead. "Generosity's never been her strong suit."

Jose gave a short laugh. "Nor ours."

Adam looked up through the hangar's transparent canopy. Above the storm clouds, a faint crescent glowed in the sky—the Moon, waiting. His pulse synced to its rhythm.

He thought of Evelyn again. The scar at the base of her skull. The way her eyes tried to be brave when the rest of her trembled. The smell of her hair in the lab—ozone and paper.

"Raptor Squad!" Osei called. "Let's remind the universe humanity still bites."

The three troopers snapped helmets into place. HUDs flared alive. Weapon systems synced with neural threads.

"Engines green," Dex said, sliding into the copilot's seat. "Jose, payload secure?"

"Locked and blessed," Jose answered.

Adam stepped into the command chair. His reflection looked back at him in the polished screen—a man who had been a dishwasher, a rescuer, a soldier, and something else now. Something born between fire and frost.

The dropship trembled as clamps released.

"Falcon's Spear, you are clear for launch," the tower intoned.

Adam closed his eyes. "Let's fly."

As Falcon's Spear broke atmosphere, the sky tore open with static. Every radio signal on Earth howled in unison. Power grids flickered and died. Cities plunged into silence.

Dex swore over comms. "EMP readings spiking. What the hell is that?"

Jose's sensors painted the Moon with infrared—the entire dark side pulsing like a living heart.

Adam stared at the feed. "The Ark."

Through the shimmer of interference, he saw it—massive, alien, alive. Spines of obsidian twisted into a ring, each vein pulsing with violet energy. Lightning crawled across its surface, silent and deliberate.

Then the static cleared just long enough for a voice to slip through the channels.

"Hello, Adam."

Victor.

Adam's blood froze. "Redmond..."

"Do you like what we've built?"

Dex's voice came sharp. "That's him, isn't it? The ghost that started this mess."

"You still think in singulars," Victor said. "One war. One world. One you. I used to."

The transmission crackled, warped by interference.

"You were the dishwasher. I was the one who cleaned the world."

Adam gritted his teeth. "You're not me."

"Oh, but I am."

The line went dead.

For a moment, no one spoke. The stars outside looked too close, as if the ship had fallen into a painting.

Then Dex broke the silence. "Well," he said quietly, "that escalated faster than a bad date."

Adam's voice was steady. "Jose, prep the drop pods. We're not turning back."

Jose nodded once. "For humanity?"

Adam checked his rifle. "For who we are."

Meanwhile — Back on Earth

In the depths of Raptor Base, Evelyn watched the comms grid collapse. One by one, the satellites went offline. The room dimmed until only her monitor glowed.

The alien code on her screen shifted, rewriting itself into symbols that looked like eyes.

"Come home," a voice whispered in her head.

She flinched, pressing her hands against the console. "No. Not again."

The waveform pulsed like a heartbeat.

"You belong to the Pattern."

She slammed a fist into the terminal. Sparks flew. The message faded—but deep in the static, she thought she heard Adam's voice counting.

Three long. Two short. One pause.

She exhaled, tears catching the light. "Hold on, Adam."

Outside, snow fell over the ice fields, glowing faintly with reflected light from the Moon—where shadows were moving.

Chapter 6

BATTLE OF APOLLO

The first thing they lost was the sky.

Every major observatory across the planet went dark within minutes.

Communications dropped. Satellites burned out one after another, leaving nothing but static.

Then came the image — a blurred transmission from the lunar array before it died: a vast black shape descending into the Moon's southern basin, unfolding like wings.

The Obsidian Ark.

Its shadow devoured the lunar horizon, drilling into the surface with spires of alien geometry.

The world's power grids faltered; electromagnetic waves bent like reeds. Within an hour, Earth was blind.

Air traffic failed. Banking systems crashed. Nations screamed into the silence.

Humanity had been thrown back into the dark.

In the command dome of Outpost Heian-Ridge, emergency lights strobed red.

Generals shouted coordinates that no longer meant anything without satellites.

Wolfgrove's voice cut through the chaos like a blade.

"Listen up! The Ark's building a facility on the Moon's far side — mining Amibian crystal, generating a signal strong enough to fry every circuit on Earth. If that facility finishes, we're done."

He turned to Raptor Squad—Adam Warn, Dex Yoi, Jose Fuentes—already suited and armed. Their armor bore new markings: a raptor's talon wrapped around a rising sun.

"Your mission is simple," Wolfgrove said. "We take the Moon. We burn the Ark."

Dex smirked. "Just three of us?"

"You'll have help," Wolfgrove said, pointing at the holo-display. Fleets of drop-cruisers and interceptors launched from orbiting stations. "You'll lead the first wave."

Reyes's absence was a shadow no one mentioned.

Evelyn stood by the transport gate, wearing a field medic's uniform. The lines under her eyes told stories of sleepless nights and survivor's guilt.

"You shouldn't be here," Adam said, fastening his helmet.

"I won't just sit and watch you die," she said.

"This isn't Earth," he replied. "It's a graveyard waiting for names. Stay here, Evelyn. Please."

She nodded, but didn't promise.

When he left, she leaned against the bulkhead, hand pressed to the back of her neck. Beneath her skin, something moved — microscopic, mechanical, whispering. A Tech-Mite, dormant no longer.

The fleet cut through the dark between worlds.

Cruisers, destroyers, and carrier ships glided in tight formation, engines glowing against the void.

Inside their drop-ship, Raptor Squad sat shoulder to shoulder. Dex hummed a tune into his helmet mic; Jose cleaned his rifle with ritual precision. Adam checked comms that crackled with static.

"Feels wrong," Jose muttered. "Like the whole universe's holding its breath."

Dex grinned. "Then let's make it exhale."

Wolfgrove's voice boomed through the channel: "Raptor Squad, you are green for drop. Bring them hell."

"Copy that," Adam said. "Raptors, on me."

The drop-pods screamed into lunar orbit, streaking fire across the gray surface.

When they hit, gravity gave them mercy — slower falls, higher leaps, every movement an echo of grace and violence.

The Moon was chaos.

Amibian Knights and Pawns swarmed across crater fields, their bioluminescent armor cutting through the darkness.

Human marines and drones advanced through plumes of regolith, rifles strobing red in the void.

Airships carved trails of plasma through the thin exosphere — fighters weaving around interceptors, bombers diving on alien towers that pulsed with unnatural light. Explosions bloomed in silence; sound couldn't follow here.

Adam vaulted a crater lip, firing bursts into a Knight's chest. The recoil sent him spinning midair; he twisted, landed on one knee, drew his blade, and sliced through a tendril arm before it could reach Dex.

Dex laughed through comms. "You're getting good at this anti-gravity thing!"

"Try not to die before I finish," Adam shot back.

Jose moved like a ghost, using the low gravity to vanish and reappear behind enemies, striking clean. One Pawn tackled him mid-leap; they crashed together, rolling through dust. Jose's blade flared — one stroke, silence.

Across the field, a human bomber plummeted, trailing fire. The crash lit the horizon like a second sun.

Above them, the fleet battle raged — humanity's airships dueling Amibian interceptors in the black.

From the Ark's hangars, squadrons of living fighters launched: coral and flesh fused, their wings beating vacuum itself. They rammed ships at suicidal speeds, detonating in bursts of green fire.

Adam caught glimpses between volleys: human pilots screaming prayers, ejecting into space where no one could hear them.

Every explosion glittered like fireworks over a graveyard.

Wolfgrove's cruiser, Titan's Mercy, took a direct hit. The comms erupted in static.

Then only Wolfgrove's voice, calm and final: "Make it count, Raptor Squad."

The signal cut.

As they all watched in Horror they had to press on.

Raptor Squad reached the Ark's surface facility — a labyrinth of black coral towers feeding power into a central spire.

Inside, the gravity shifted between zero and too much.

Pawns clung to walls like insects; Knights fired shards of molten plasma.

Dex hacked into a console mid-firefight. "If I reroute the lunar drills, we can overload their core!"

"Do it!" Adam shouted.

Jose covered him, cutting through two charging Pawns. The third impaled him through the shoulder; Jose roared, pulled the spear deeper to get close enough to decapitate his attacker.

Adam fought like a storm, moving faster than physics had patience for. TURBO mode blurred time again — every heartbeat a lifetime.

He reached the spire, planted the detonation charge, and saw something that stopped him.

A human ship had landed nearby. A small one. A medic's cruiser.

Evelyn.

She stumbled through the chaos, carrying a med-pack, shouting his name.

He reached her, grabbed her shoulders. "Evelyn—what are you doing here?"

"I couldn't stay behind," she said, eyes shining. "You need me."

Before he could answer, her expression changed.

She winced, pressing her hand to her neck. Under her skin, something crawled.

Adam's blood froze. "No..."

The Tech-Mite burst its whisper into the comm channel, distorting her voice into a thousand echoes of Nyarlathotep's laughter.

She came to you, Adam Warn. I sent her. The pattern completes.

Her scream cut through the static.

Dex's voice thundered through the channel. "Charge set! We have to go!"

Adam looked at Evelyn, trembling, light spilling from her eyes.

He pulled her close. "I'll save you. I swear it."

She shook her head, tears glowing in zero-G. "Save them."

The charge went off.

Light devoured the horizon.

The Ark's lunar facility shattered, molten shards raining into the void.

The shockwave rippled across the Moon, carving a new crater visible from Earth.

Raptor Squad's escape pods ejected just before the surface collapsed.

The Moon burned.

From Earth, people looked up and saw the silver disk scarred black, a wound that would never heal.

Communications flickered back for a moment — enough to confirm victory.

But the war was far from over.

Half the fleet gone. Half the soldiers dead.

Wolfgrove's sacrifice.

And Evelyn—lost to something worse than death.

Adam sat in silence inside the escape pod, helmet cracked, hands trembling. Dex's voice came through weakly, "We did it, man... the Moon's ours."

Adam stared at the distant Earth, a blue sphere still burning at the edges.

"Not yet," he said. "Not until it stops screaming."

Chapter 7

THE MIRROR AND THE FLAME

.

The Moon was still burning when they came.

Raptor Squad's escape pod had crashed into a crater near the ruins of the Obsidian facility. Smoke and dust drifted into the endless void.

Adam climbed free, coughing through the crack in his helmet.

"Dex? Jose?"

Static answered.

He saw movement through the gray haze—a human silhouette staggering across the ridge.

Evelyn.

He started toward her, heart hammering. Before he could reach her, a Knight burst from the dust, its four arms gripping her like a doll. Her scream tore through the comm channel.

"EVELYN!"

The Knight shoved her into his ship—and it launched upward toward orbit, carrying her into the dark. Behind it, an Amibian interceptor streaked free of the debris field, engines glowing sickly green.

Adam ran, lungs raw, boots slipping on glassed lunar rock. His suit's oxygen warning screamed. He didn't care.

He found a wrecked human interceptor half-buried nearby—pilot dead, canopy cracked, systems flickering weak blue.

He climbed in, ripped the pilot's body free, sealed the hatch, and shouted into his mic.

"This is Raptor One! Pursuing target outbound! Evelyn's been taken!"

No response. Earth and the fleet were silent.

He gunned the engines anyway.

"Come on…" he muttered, hands trembling on the controls.

He fired the interceptor's grappling harpoon—a magnetic tether used for ship repair—at the fleeing Amibian craft. It caught, sparking against alien hull metal.

Alarms blared as the tether pulled him into the Ark's atmosphere shield, friction plasma turning the cockpit white-hot.

He ejected at the last second.

The impact threw him through a maintenance corridor, armor scraping sparks off coral-steel walls. The ship shuddered underfoot—a living heartbeat echoing through the hull.

He stood, sword drawn, rifle low on charge.

Somewhere inside this monster, she was alive.

Footsteps.

Echoes on metal.

He turned a corner—and froze.

A figure stood at the end of the corridor.

Tall, armored in obsidian and silver, half flesh, half machine.

A crimson glow under one eye, the other unmistakably human.

"Adam Warn," the man said.

The voice was his own—older, colder, sharpened into command.

"Who are you?" Adam demanded.

"You already know."

The figure drew a sword forged of pure light—its blade humming with an Amibian resonance Adam recognized from his own.

Victor Redmond.

Their swords met with a sound that split the air—a chime that wasn't sound so much as vibration.

Adam lunged, fast and raw. Victor parried with mechanical precision, sparks flaring off the walls.

"You fight like me," Victor said, smiling without warmth. "Unrefined, but familiar."

"I'm not you."

"You're exactly me. You just haven't learned it yet."

Adam feinted low, kicked Victor backward, then slammed his blade into the floor and used the rebound to strike again.

Victor caught the blow with his cybernetic arm; metal screamed, then he twisted, disarming Adam and hurling him into a wall.

"Your world still fights for order," Victor said. "Mine already lost it. We're not so different—you just haven't buried your gods yet."

Adam spat blood, eyes blazing. "You killed mine when you came here."

Victor tilted his head. "Not yet. But I will."

They clashed again. The Ark itself seemed to breathe with each strike—corridors flexing, walls pulsing in rhythm with their movements.

Adam caught Victor's shoulder, sparks flying as he cut through layers of armor and flesh. Black liquid—half oil, half blood—splashed across the deck.

Victor didn't flinch. "Good. Anger looks good on you."

He struck back, blade across Adam's chestplate. Systems screamed red. Adam fell to one knee.

Victor raised his sword for the killing blow—then stopped.

"Not yet," he said softly. "You still have a part to play. The girl is mine now. And soon... you'll beg me to end you."

A blast rocked the corridor—Dex's voice crackling through Adam's comm. "Hey, boss! You alive in there? Because I just bombed a goddamn hole in their hangar!"

Victor turned toward the noise. "Your friends arrived early. How fortunate."

He stepped backward into a shaft of violet light. "This isn't over."

"Evelyn!" Adam shouted, pushing himself upright.

Victor's smile was faint and cruel. "She's already halfway home."

Then he was gone—swallowed by the light, leaving the corridor cracked and burning.

Adam limped toward the breach where the Ark's hull had ruptured. He could see the fleet outside, a chaotic ballet of burning ships and drifting debris.

Dex's dropship swung close, side hatch open.

"Move your ass, Idiot—sorry, I mean Adam!" Dex yelled.

Adam dove for the hatch just as the Ark's defense batteries reactivated. The explosion hurled the ship outward, tumbling through vacuum toward the stars.

Inside, Dex grabbed him, slammed the hatch shut, and sealed the pressure. "You look like shit, man."

"She's gone," Adam rasped.

Dex's grin faded. "We'll get her back."

Adam stared out the viewport as the Obsidian Ark receded into the distance—a bleeding wound against the stars.

"We will," he said quietly. "Even if I have to tear it apart with my hands."

Chapter 8

THE HOLLOW BETWEEN WORLDS

The Obsidian Ark hung in lunar shadow, half-lit by the ruined Moon it had scarred. Inside its black corridors, the air shimmered with whispers—metal and something older than time.

Evelyn Lu woke on a table of liquid glass. Tubes fed into her veins; faint blue circuits pulsed beneath her skin. Her vision swam, her breath catching in artificial rhythm.

"Easy," a voice said.

Victor Redmond stepped from the gloom, half man, half monument. His cybernetic frame gleamed under cold light. One eye flickered red; the other, human, watched her with unreadable calm.

"Where... am I?" she rasped.

"Inside the Ark," he said. "Inside me, if you want to be poetic."

She tried to sit up—restraints hissed. Beneath her skin, the Tech-Mite writhed, tiny filaments weaving through her nerves. She felt it whispering—not in words but in pulses, like someone tapping code against her spine.

Victor studied a holomap of her vitals. "Remarkable. Your body fights it—rejects my design. Adam always did prefer the stubborn ones."

At the sound of that name she stiffened. "Where is he?"

"Alive. For now." Victor looked up, expression softening almost like pity. "He doesn't understand yet. What I am. What he is."

"What are you talking about?"

He didn't answer. Instead he pressed a finger to the glass beside her face. The wall came alive—showing Earth below, cities flickering in blackout, wars burning across continents.

"Do you hear it?" he asked. "The silence between signals? The world gasping for order? I gave up my soul to stop that sound. He still clings to it."

"You're insane," she whispered.

Victor smiled. "No. I'm evolved. Nyarlathotep showed me what unity truly means—one voice, one pattern. You and Adam could have been the seed of that perfection."

He leaned close; his breath smelled faintly of metal and ozone. "Instead, you'll help me finish it."

He pressed his palm to her chest. The Tech-Mite surged. Evelyn screamed—light pouring from her eyes as the parasite rewrote her blood.

The Ark echoed with her cry. Somewhere in its depths, something vast and patient laughed.

Earth Orbit — Three Days Later

Raptor Squad's transport limped through the upper atmosphere trailing fire. Inside, the air stank of coolant and blood.

Dex lay strapped to a gurney, half his armor melted into his shoulder. Jose sat nearby, arm in a sling, eyes fixed on nothing.

Adam stood at the viewport, his reflection ghosting over the planet's haze of smoke and aurora-fire.

The radio crackled weakly.

"...Earth Command to surviving units—report... casualties exceed seventy percent... global communications offline..."

Jose muttered, "We win a battle, lose a planet."

Dex coughed a laugh. "We always did have bad luck."

Adam didn't turn. "It's not luck. It's strategy. His."

Wolfgrove was gone. Reyes was gone. Evelyn was gone. Every voice that used to tell him why was fading. All that remained was the hum—the same low pattern that had haunted him since childhood, now threading through every transmission like static that refused to die.

Jose glanced up. "You good, brother?"

Adam exhaled. "No. But I'm still standing."

Dex managed a grin. "Then we stand with you."

Their ship touched down in what had once been Outpost Kilim Base, now a crater rimmed with burned tanks and frozen corpses. The sky above was orange with debris, the Moon a scarred crescent overhead.

Soldiers scavenged through ruins, salvaging power cells to keep the lights alive.

Someone played an old radio quietly—crackling static between half-songs. The sound reminded Adam of home.

He stared up at the Moon, where the Ark's shadow still lingered. "He's building something bigger. The Tech-Mites... Evelyn..."

Dex pushed himself upright, grimacing through pain. "Then we build faster. Smarter."

Jose nodded. "We hit him before he hits us again."

Adam closed his eyes. Behind the darkness, he saw flashes of her face, the movement beneath her skin, the glow of her scream.

He whispered to himself, almost a prayer. "Hold on, Eve. I'm coming."

Aboard the Ark

Victor stood at a viewport overlooking Earth. Evelyn floated in a containment field behind him, unconscious, threads of light still coiling under her skin. The infection had stopped spreading—but her heartbeat pulsed in sync with the Ark's engines.

Nyarlathotep's presence stirred through the walls like static through bone.

The pattern aligns, the god said. The mirror is cracking.

Victor bowed his head slightly. "He's chasing us."

"Good. Let him follow. The stronger he fights the current, the deeper he drowns."

Victor looked down at the world below, at the fires and blackouts. "He'll come for her. And when he does, the door between our worlds will finally open."

He smiled faintly, the same smile Adam wore when he believed.

"Then we'll both be free."

The Ark's lights dimmed. Engines shifted tone—lower, older. The ship turned toward Earth.

Chapter 9

GRAVES IN ORBIT

The med-frigate hums like a stalled hymn. Bulkheads whisper with the voices of the wounded—soft, ragged, unfinished. Outside the narrow viewport, Earth rolls beneath like a bruised eye. Beyond it, the Moon is wrong: a crescent with a bite taken out, dark regolith torn into floating ribs, bright veins of vapor venting into the black.

Adam wakes to the antiseptic sting of recycled air and the weight of straps across his chest. HUD ghosting lingers in his eyes—numbers that aren't there, warnings that never stop blinking. He breathes. Counts. Three long. Two short. One pause. The rhythm steadies his hands.

"You looked worse than the Moon, Ronin." Dex sits in the chair by his cot, sling crooked, lip split. He tries a grin that doesn't make it to his eyes. "And the Moon is currently auditioning for 'corpse.'"

Adam swallows. His throat tastes like copper and oxygen. "We make it?"

"We didn't die," Dex says. "That's not the same thing, but it'll pass inspection." He leans forward, elbows on knees. "Welcome back to orbit."

Jose stands by the viewport, a hard silhouette against the soft wash of planetlight. He has a small notepad—real paper, torn and frayed—and he's writing names in a steady, careful hand. The list is longer than a page. He turns it without looking up.

Adam shifts, the straps rasping. "Reyes?"

Dex's grin leaves completely. Jose closes the notebook and slips it into his breast pocket, thumb resting on the crease like a benediction.

"We keep her," Jose says. Voice even. "Not the body. The order."

The frantic orchestra of the ward swells and ebbs: med-drones clicking past, the hoarse cough of a burned throat, a whispered prayer in a language Adam doesn't know. He studies the blue seam of Earth's atmosphere and wants to feel hope. What he feels is distance.

A medic appears, scans Adam's ports, murmurs something about neural overload and TURBO residue, then leaves a cup of water and a vial of bitter pills. Adam doesn't touch the pills. He drinks, slow. The water rattles in the paper cup.

Dex toes a crate until it yields three dented ration cans and a squat bottle that someone smuggled aboard in a toolkit. "Don't ask what it is. The label only says 'Don't.'" He opens it anyway, pours into metal caps. The smell is industrial, a solvent that remembers being a fruit.

"To Reyes," Dex says, lifting his cap.

Jose joins them at the cot. He nods once. "To the man who believed we could be better than what we were built for."

Adam raises his cap. The liquid bites. Heat runs a wire through his chest. They drink in silence. Somewhere, a heart monitor flatlines, then stutters back into life. Somewhere else, a nurse laughs, too loud, and puts a hand over her mouth as if she's broken a rule.

They sit with the burn a while. Dex sets his cap on the floor and tips it with two fingers, as if the floor were a grave.

"Debrief in an hour," he says. "HQ wants a fairytale about miracles. We don't have one, so we'll tell the truth in a way that looks like lying."

Jose's jaw flexes. "We lost a carrier over Mare Tranquillitatis. Two hundred and eleven confirmed. Fifty-eight unconfirmed." He doesn't open the notebook. He doesn't have to. "We saved the rest. That's the part I'm choosing."

Adam's hands find the edges of the cot. He remembers the way the lunar dust hung in the vacuum like smoke that refused to descend; remembers the Knight's arm crushing across his visor; remembers Dex's hand where there shouldn't have been time for one. He remembers Evelyn's voice through the static like a candle in rain.

"She's on the Ark," he says.

Dex rubs at his face, pauses when the sling complains. "Or something wearing her shape. You know what I mean."

"I know what I heard."

Jose looks out at the planet. The med-frigate drifts into Earth's shadow; city lights prick the dark like stitched wounds. Then, blot by blot, whole swaths of the world wink out. The ward murmurs as the newsfeeds catch up.

"Comms are falling," Dex mutters. "Sat grids are cooked. They hit our eyes, our ears, our mouths."

The bulkhead screen over Adam's cot flares awake, no one touching it. An automatic disaster rotation plays: grainy feeds of coastlines garrisoned by Amibian scaffolds, coral-black pylons sprouting around harbors; highways clotted with stalled cars, doors open, hazard lights blinking in empty lanes; soldiers fighting in stadiums because stadiums are the only places left that can hold what's happening. A camera catches an Amibian Pawn lifting a man as casually as someone lifts a jacket—five-and-a-half feet of muscle and coral armor—then tossing him into a wall with the bored power of weather. Another clip shows a Knight wading through a barricade, eight feet of velvet savagery, four arms working like a factory, lifting a truck and setting it aside as if rearranging furniture.

Dex kills the feed with a slap of his palm. "We won a rock and lost a planet."

Adam breathes through his teeth. He wants to be moving. Forward, through, toward. The straps feel like webbing. He remembers a sink full of plates. He remembers a plastic apron that smelled like lemon and yeast.

"It's still about who we are," he says. "That hasn't changed."

Jose studies him. "Maybe it's about what's left."

"Then what's left has to matter." He hears his father's voice in the echo, calm and stubborn: Every machine has a pattern, son. Listen and you'll know how to fix it.

Dex looks between them. "What's left is three idiots and a ship with a personality disorder, plus a general who thinks sarcasm is a fuel." He points at Adam's chest. "And a reactor in your head that keeps trying to melt you."

"I'm fine."

"You're cooked," Dex says, not unkindly. "You stared through the wall for ten minutes before you realized I was in the room."

Adam doesn't deny it. The after-hum of TURBO crawls under his skin like cold light. He can still see edges too clearly. He can still imagine the fraction of a second where the blade splits a neck and wonder who he's going to be when that second's over.

The deck plates shiver. Not an impact. A pulse. It moves through the ship like a slow wave. The fluorescents flicker. The med-drones' eyes cycle and reset.

"EMP?" Dex asks.

The intercom chirps: "All hands—hold positions. Repeat: hold positions."

The pulse fades. The fluorescents steady.

A young lieutenant stumbles into their aisle, cheeks wind-burned by radiation and responsibility. "Raptor Squad—Command wants you in CIC. Now."

"See?" Dex says, standing with a sigh. "Sarcasm is a fuel."

They move through the ward like ghosts—careful not to touch too much, to snag their grief on anyone else's. The CIC sits at the spine of the frigate, a ring of consoles beneath a dome that projects war onto the ceiling like sacrilege. General Osei is there, hands on the tactical rail, face carved from the kind of patience that bleeds.

"Sit," she says. No one does. "Fine. Look."

The dome shows the Ark's wreckage field beyond the Moon—a halo of black geometry drifting in a thin glitter of ice and dust. Energy readings spasm in sickly violet. The largest fragment rotates, revealing a lattice of hexagons that occasionally line up and flash in a way that feels like blinking.

"It's not dead," Dex says.

"It's hungry," Jose replies.

Osei gestures. Another feed opens—this one from deep-spectrum receivers along the frigate's hull. Not sound, not really—an oscillation rendered so humans can stand to consume it. It's a pattern: three long, two short, one pause. Then again. Then twice as fast.

Adam's heart lurches into sync without asking permission.

"Signal repeats every forty-seven seconds," Osei says. "The first layer is a wide-band jamming field. Buried under it—this." She nods to the comms officer, who isolates and amplifies. The oscillation resolves into a waveform like a heartbeat and a spectrogram like handwriting.

"Voiceprint," the comms officer says. "Layered. Corrupted. But the core signature matches a civilian we have on file. Evelyn Lu."

Dex closes his eyes. "Dammit."

"Is it live?" Adam asks.

"We don't know," Osei says. "It could be an echo. A trap. It could be a recording waiting for anything with ears. But if it's a lure, it's an expensive one. The enemy is bleeding power to keep it transmitting."

The Ark fragment blinks again. Adam's throat tightens. He pictures Evelyn in the lab, her hands over the console as if it were a wound she could close with pressure. He pictures her eyes when she said You still talk like the world can be fixed.

"What do you need from us?" he asks.

Osei's mouth goes thin. "A recon run was going to be somone's suicide. I prefer volunteers." She doesn't look away. "Before you mouth the word, Dexter, remember that your last three 'volunteer' operations ended in disciplinary reviews and medals that no one wants to wear."

Dex spreads his good hand. "I was only going to ask if the medals come in black."

Jose touches the rail. "We go. We don't stay long. We bring back what we can carry."

"Or who," Adam says.

Osei studies him a heartbeat too long. "If she's alive, she's not alone. If you find her, you'll find them."

"Them," Dex repeats. "It's always the useful pronouns with you."

Osei lifts her chin toward the dome. The Ark fragment spins, a cathedral of angles swallowing starlight. "There's something else. We pulled telemetry from the last minutes of the lunar engagement." She exhales through her nose. "The Ark isn't just a ship. It's eating."

Dex frowns. "Eating what."

"The Moon," Osei says simply. "Core metals. Heat. Mass. It's been threading the regolith for months. We only saw the sprouts."

The CIC goes quiet in a way machinery tries to imitate. Adam sees the pattern again, not as mercy or inevitability, but as appetite in the shape of geometry.

"Gear within the hour," Osei says. "Falcon's Spear is fueled. If you're going, go fast."

They file out on the last words. In the corridor, Dex falls into step beside Adam, voice low. "You sure you can fly without melting?"

"I won't melt," Adam says.

"You will lie to me," Dex says. "It's in your job description."

Jose walks on Adam's other side. "He will not melt," he says, the way some men say Amen.

The hangar opens like a mouth. Crews swarm Falcon's Spear with the choreography of people who turned fear into work a long time ago. The ship crouches like it's ready to spring. Adam palms the boarding ramp and feels the metal recognize him.

"Five minutes," a tech yells. "Or you're watching from the window."

"Wouldn't dream of it," Dex says, already halfway up the ramp.

Adam lingers just long enough to look back down the corridor. He imagines Evelyn there, just around the bend, hair pulled back, eyes rimmed with sleeplessness and light. He imagines telling her something ordinary: I'll be right back. He imagines her not believing him and forgiving him anyway.

A tremor picks the soles of his feet up, sets them down again. Not the ship. The pattern. Three long. Two short. One pause. The Ark fragment blinking like an animal that remembers before it learned to fear.

They strap in. Systems wake. The cockpit washes blue. Dex runs through the checklist with one hand, the other pressed to his ribs like he's holding something in.

"Jose?"

"Payload green."

"Ronin?"

Adam feels the old chair in his head—the imagined seat where he learned to breathe while the world shouted. He sits there an instant, in the quiet, and then stands out of it, because quiet is a story they don't get to keep.

"Ready," he says.

Falcon's Spear lifts on a column of light, turns its nose toward the wound in the sky, and goes.

The med-frigate falls behind, a bright island in a black sea. Earth turns its wounded face away. The Moon waits, less a place than a warning. Between them, the Ark fragment spins, and in its pulse a voice hides like a shard of glass in clean water.

It comes in at the edge of hearing, woven under the jamming hiss, a syllable stretched thin as wire.

"Adam."

He closes his eyes, counts once, and opens them on the dark.

"If there's even a chance it's her," he says into the comm, to the ship, to the universe that keeps demanding proof of love, "I'm going back."

Chapter 10

THE COSMIC PHOBIA

The airlock hisses open with a sharp exhale, and the Moon swallows the sound whole.

No wind.

No generator hum.

No radio chatter.

Only the dry rasp of respirators and the dull, pressurized pounding of heartbeat inside helmets.

Adam steps out first.

The dust takes flight in slow, drifting sheets. Each particle glows softly under their helmet lamps, floating in lazy arcs before settling again. The lunar base sprawls ahead—silent, gutted, and burnt from the inside like a corpse with its marrow scorched away. Floodlights that should be blazing across the crater are black. Consoles are dead. Even the stars above feel muted, swallowed by a vast, suffocating stillness.

Dex mutters, "Place looks like God forgot to hit save."

Jose doesn't laugh.

Nobody does.

Evelyn walks between them, her posture too stiff, too precise—like a marionette being led by invisible strings. Her visor reflects the ruins ahead: twisted beams, collapsed corridors, and floating debris drifting in the low gravity like funeral ash.

Adam keeps glancing back at her.

No one else cares she's back or alive.

Something in her gait is wrong.

Something in her breathing is wrong.

Something inside her... isn't her.

His chest tightens.

He shakes it off and moves deeper into the base.

Inside, the silence grows heavy. Smothering. Predatory.

The hallway is cylindrical and long, lined with cryo glass and shattered monitors. Blood beads float midair like suspended rubies. A soldier drifts past them, limbs stiff and rigid, faceplate cracked from the inside as if something tried to claw its way out.

His eyes—frozen wide—stare directly through Adam, unblinking.

Jose whispers, "Tech-Mite did that."

Adam swallows. "We don't know that."

But they do.

Everyone does.

The Tech-Mite victims never die quietly. They die thinking. Screaming. The parasite rides the brain like reins on a dying animal, bending bodies until bone gives way and organs tear loose.

Dex forces steadiness into his voice. "Let's keep moving. And let's not... touch anything."

They push forward.

Emergency lights flicker overhead in a stuttering rhythm. Shadows stretch too long, too thin, too aware. Adam's HUD crackles—static, blackout, static again.

Comms drop into dead silence.

Gravity hums... then stutters.

The floor pulls at them, then releases suddenly, tossing the squad upward. They float—then slam back down.

Adam hits the deck hard, knee clanging against metal. "System interference. Something's broadcasting."

Jose grabs his arm and steadies him. "Something alive?"

"No," Adam says. "Something moving."

They round a corner.

And freeze.

The research chamber is a tomb of horrors.

Bodies hang from the ceiling, cocooned in a thick, organic filament—pale, veined sacks of armor and flesh and cables fused together. Some twitch. Some pulse. Some... gape open, hollow, emptied.

The room reeks of copper and something sweet, rotten, fermented.

Dex's breath hitches. "What... the hell is this?"

Jose raises his rifle. "Experiments."

But Adam moves closer.

His fingertips shake against the rifle grip.

Inside one of the cocoons, bound into a web of spinal wires and bio-circuits, a soldier's eye flicks open.

It rolls toward Adam—desperate, pleading.

Their chest barely rises, lungs crushed under the webbing.

They try to scream.

Only a thin wheeze escapes.

Adam stumbles back.

The lights shudder.

And Evelyn... smiles.

Just barely.

Small.

Delighted.

Like she's watching something beautiful unfold.

The smile is gone the instant Adam turns toward her.

He forces himself to speak. "Evelyn? You okay?"

She tilts her head. Slow. Too slow. Mechanical. Her visor catches a strip of light that looks like a vertical pupil glinting across the mask.

"I'm fine," she says.

But the cadence.

The rhythm.

The lack of breath behind the words.

It's wrong. Too even. Too rehearsed.

Like a synthetic voice wearing human skin.

Adam steps closer. "Eve... look at me."

She does.

Her visor flickers with a faint orange glow—internal data streams bleeding through.

Adam's stomach drops. "Your HUD is—"

"I said I'm fine."

Her voice is hers.

But rebuilt.

Artificially smoothed.

Like someone copied the waveform and pressed it through a digital mold.

Dex whisper-shouts, "Guys... ceiling."

Something scuttles across the dome above them.

Metal claws scraping.

Wet joints clicking.

Flesh dragging across steel.

The creature moves in a spiral, clinging upside down with too many limbs. A Tech-Mite drone—half machine, half living tissue—glides over the ceiling panels, its head a warped fusion of twisted metal and a screaming human face frozen mid-agony.

It halts directly above Evelyn.

Adam raises his rifle. "Move!"

Evelyn doesn't.

The drone lowers its mandibles.

A wet, splitting shriek tears through the chamber.

It drops.

Jose fires first. Dex second. Adam third.

The drone hits the floor and folds in on itself—twisting, spasming, refusing to die as its nerves misfire.

Adam spins toward Evelyn. "Why didn't you move?!"

She tilts her head—curious, studying him. "I didn't need to."

Jose whispers, "Adam... who are you talking to?"

Adam feels the words like a knife sliding under his ribs.

He grabs Evelyn's shoulders. "Eve, look at me. Please—look at me. Are you hurt?"

Evelyn lifts her visor.

And for a single heartbeat—just one—Adam sees it.

Something small. Metallic.

Crawling beneath her skin.

A thin silhouette sliding along her cheekbone toward her temple.

His heart stops cold.

"Eve..."

Her pupils dilate.

Shrink.

Dilate again.

A pulsing cycle—too fast, too exact to be human.

She whispers, "It's so quiet here."

Adam's breath trembles. "What did they do to you?"

She leans in until her helmet presses against his.

"They opened my mind."

Her voice has an edge—sharp, cold, alien.

Dex steps forward, rifle half-raised. "Adam. She's dead, that's not Evelyn"

Evelyn's head snaps toward Dex.

Not a turn.

A jerk, like a predator scenting prey.

Her whisper is not human:

"I Love You..."

The lights die.

Total blackness collapses around them.

Only Adam's ragged breath moves the air.

And Evelyn's voice—sweet, loving, and entirely wrong—drifts through the dark:

"Adam... stay with me."

Only the three and carcasses of the dead were around, Adam was only holding an echo of what Evelyn was becoming.

Chapter 11

THE WITCHING SIGNAL

The Ark Starship drifts above the Moon like a cathedral built from dead stars. Its hull plates are carved with Amibian script—etched in bone and metal, pulsing faintly with cosmic energy. Every surface hums with pressure, like something inside the ship wants to scream.

Victor Redmond stands on the command dais, cloak billowing in the recycled draft of the central reactor. His cybernetic half glimmers in the dim, blood-orange lights. The ship's psionic relay feeds directly into the ports along the side of his skull, bathing his mind in streams of data.

But Victor only watches one thing:

Evelyn.

Her image flickers in a floating hologram—her visor trembling with static, her posture rigid, her silhouette haloed in emergency strobe light. Her breath loops in a glitched cycle: inhale, glitch, inhale again, exhale too slowly.

Victor stares at her as one would stare at a portrait of someone long dead.

"She looks just like you, Jay," he murmurs.

A creeping mechanical chime echoes as a Amibian officer approaches—its four arms folded behind its armored torso, its six eyes blinking out of sequence.

"Lord Redmond," it hisses. "Subject 07 resists integration. The neural invasion encounters emotional anchors."

Victor's human eye grows distant. The cybernetic one sharpens.

"Emotional anchors." He tastes the words like poison. "Of course she has them."

He steps down from the dais, boots clanging against the latticework floor.

"Jay had them too."

The officer tilts its cephalopod-like head. "Jay Aguilar. Deceased—"

Victor's voice slices through the chamber.

"Do not speak her name."

The officer bows, cowed.

Victor turns back to the hologram. Evelyn twitches as though something drags her head by invisible hooks. Her visor distorts—her reflection shatters like broken glass.

Adam's voice crackles faintly in the uplink, distorted by lunar interference:

"Eve—look at me! Please—"

Victor inhales sharply through his teeth.

He whispers, "He always knew how to say her name."

The officer shifts uneasily. "Subject 07's memories accelerate corruption. Her affection for the target weakens the parasite's efficiency."

Victor's jaw flexes. "Affection."

He spits the word.

"You think I don't know what affection looks like? You think I didn't feel it when Jay smiled at me on the front lines? Before the world burned? Before I sold my soul to keep something alive?"

The officer does not respond.

Victor steps close to the hologram, tracing the edge of Evelyn's projected cheek with a metal fingertip.

"She could have been Jay in another life. In another timeline. A universe where I didn't lose everything."

He lowers his hand.

"But Adam gets that universe. Adam. Not me."

He turns, cloak snapping behind him.

"Increase the signal strength."

"My lord... her mind may not hold."

"She doesn't have to hold," Victor snaps. "She just has to break the right way."

The officer bows again and hurries off.

Victor moves deeper into the Ark, passing beneath archways built from interlocking Amibian bone. The walls pulse with bioluminescent veins, each beat resonating through the hull like the breath of a slumbering god.

A whisper crawls across Victor's thoughts.

Deep.

Cold.

Ancient.

"Feed her mind... to me."

Victor bows his head slightly. "Yes, Master."

He walks into the central reactor chamber—the heart of the Ark—a colossal sphere suspended in a cradle of obsidian and tentacular metal. The sphere is half-machine, half-organism, throbbing with energy that bends the air around it.

Nyarlathotep's presence stirs inside.

A low tremble ripples through the deck. Panels flicker. The distant wails of Amibian priest-engineers echo through the halls.

Victor breathes deeply.

"This world will break just like mine did," he says quietly. "But this time... I determine what rises from the ashes."

A nearby display lights up in response to his voice.

"Show me Adam Warn."

The hologram shifts.

Adam appears—helmet steaming with condensation, rifle raised, heart pounding so hard it shakes the HUD feed. Dust swirls around him. His voice, distorted but unmistakably frantic:

"Evelyn! Evelyn, answer me!"

Victor stares at him.

"I died on a train," he whispers. "In my world... I fell into fire. Into chaos. Into the dark. And the universe birthed me again with metal bones and a hollow heart."

He steps closer, eyes narrowing.

"You lived. You survived your father's death. Your mother leaving. You were loved. You were understood."

His voice trembles with fury.

"Why do you get to be whole?"

His cybernetic eye pulses red.

"And why does she love you?"

The hologram flickers.

Evelyn stares back at him—eyes dilating, shrinking, cycling, trying to resist.

Victor feels her push back through the Tech-Mite uplink.

A whisper of her real voice.

Soft.

Terrified.

"Adam... please..."

Victor clenches his jaw as her fear leaks into his mind. For a moment, he feels her pain.

Her memories.

Her childhood.

Her loneliness.

Her hope.

Jay's memories echo through her.

Jay's smile.

Jay's warmth.

Victor staggers. His breath quickens.

"No," he growls. "Not yours. Not for him."

He slams his palm against the control surface.

"Boost the psychic override!"

A lab of Tech-Mite engineers—twitching, half-conscious, wired into machines—obey instantly. The uplink hums like a swarm of metal insects.

Evelyn screams—not aloud, but through Victor's skull, raw and electronic.

Victor shudders.

"That's it," he whispers. "Break. Shatter. Bring him to me."

The officer approaches again, trembling. "Lord Redmond... the fleets await command."

Victor straightens.

"Deploy all Knight units to Earth orbit. Darken the lunar grid. Collapse their satellites. Prepare the dimensional aperture for phase three."

The officer bows.

Victor raises his hand.

"And give Subject 07 one last command."

"What command, my lord?"

Victor stares at Adam's hologram—his dimensional twin, his reflection across universes.

His voice is cold.

"Call him by his name."

He turns toward the massive viewport.

Earth rotates beneath the Ark—blue, bright, blind to its coming doom.

Victor whispers:

"Adam Warn. Come find her."

The Ark's engines ignite, flooding the chamber with hellish light.

"And when you do... find me."

Chapter 12

WHITE RABBIT

The world reappears in shards of white and burning orange.

Adam's HUD explodes back to life—flickering, glitching, overloaded with warnings—and the stuttering emergency lights in the lunar corridor pulse like a dying heart. The floor trembles beneath him. Dust floats in torn, drifting ribbons.

Dex grabs his shoulder. "Adam! Snap out of it—we gotta move!"

Adam stands at the threshold of the room, rifle up, breath ragged through the comms. "Where is Evelyn?!"

Adam spins—

And feels a void inside his chest.

She's gone.

The air tastes hollow.

The silence feels predatory.

He raises his voice, already knowing she cannot hear him.

"EVELYN!"

His scream travels down the corridor, bouncing off metal ribs and broken conduit.

A second tremor hits—stronger. The walls buckle. Cocooned bodies sway violently above them, suspended in the sagging cables.

One breaks free from the ceiling—

A soldier fused with Tech-Mite wires—

And drifts toward them, twitching like a marionette cut from its strings.

Jose instinctively fires.

The cocoon ruptures in a wet burst.

Metal and fluid float, sparkling in the low gravity.

Dex curses. "We're out of time!"

They run.

The hallway collapses behind them in sections, each implosion sending slow-motion debris swirling through the air like a silent storm. Tech-Mite drones spill from broken vents, crawling across the walls like metallic insects.

One leaps onto Jose's back—

Adam grabs its leg, rips it free, crushes it under his boot until it spasms into silence.

Jose grunts. "Thanks..."

Adam nods, breath shaking. "We keep moving."

Dex glances at him as they run. "We're gonna find her, Adam. I swear."

Adam doesn't answer.

But his silence says everything.

The final airlock looms ahead.

Lights flicker and die.

The floor hums and then goes weightless.

Adam, Dex, and Jose float upward—

Then slam back down.

Alarms blare.

CORE STRUCTURE FAILURE.

PHASE TWO INITIATED.

ALL ORGANIC MATTER WILL BE PROCESSED.

Dex spits, "I hate this place!"

Jose braces the door. "Override it!"

"I'm trying!" Dex slams his gauntlet into the panel.

A shriek splits the air—

A Tech-Mite drone crawls along the ceiling, slamming into the wall sideways like a broken spider, limbs clicking wildly.

Adam's pulse spikes.

He fires.

The drone explodes into shattered bone-mech fragments.

The door finally grinds open.

They burst onto the lunar surface—

And the world changes.

The Moon is no longer silent.

It is alive with war.

Burning trails streak across the starfield as Amibian dreadnoughts descend like gods of steel and bone. Carriers shaped like colossal armored cephalopods unfold their limbs, releasing swarms of interceptors. Blue-white beams slice through the vacuum, carving trenches of glowing glass into the lunar surface.

Dex freezes. "Holy... hell."

Jose's jaw clenches. "Earth's next."

And then—

Earth flickers.

The entire planet dims.

Lights wink out along its nightside—

satellites bursting in silent explosions,

defense arrays shattering like brittle porcelain,

networks collapsing in cascading failures.

Adam steps forward, heart pounding.

"Reyes... Command... everyone. They're blind."

Then—

Evelyn's voice whispers inside his helmet.

Not through comms.

Through something else.

"Adam..."

He freezes.

Dex and Jose look at him instantly.

"Adam?" Dex asks. "What is it?"

Adam barely breathes. "Her."

Jose steps closer. "What did she say?"

Adam's shoulders shake. "That she's still in there."

Dex puts a hand on Adam's arm. "Then we're getting her back. No matter what."

The crater shakes.

An Amibian Knight drop-pod slams into the ground nearby, unfolding its metal legs like a blooming metal flower. A Knight emerges—towering, blue-armored, carrying a blade the size of a car's hood.

Jose aims. "Contact!"

Adam raises a hand. "No. Not here."

Jose stares. "What? It's right there!"

Adam turns. His voice is different now—

sharp, commanding, fueled by something deeper than rage.

"We don't waste time. We need a ship."

Dex nods. "The debris fields might have one intact."

Jose grins faintly. "Stealing an enemy ship. Classic Raptor Squad."

Adam steps toward the crater's edge.

His armor glows faintly under the twin lights of the Earth and the burning dreadnoughts.

He whispers to himself:

"Evelyn... I'm coming."

They sprint across the crater toward the warfront.

Lunar dust explodes beneath their boots. Shockwaves ripple in long, slow undulations. Amibian interceptors swoop overhead, firing lances of plasma that carve glowing arcs across the surface.

A damaged human interceptor spirals down and impacts a ridge—

Adam sprints toward it, sliding down the slope.

Inside, a dying pilot reaches toward him.

Adam grabs his hand.

The pilot wheezes, "Warn... the fleet is gone... they burned us out of orbit..."

Adam sets him down gently. "Rest now."

The pilot's hand slips from Adam's grip.

Silence.

Adam stands.

Dex and Jose stand beside him—one on each side.

Dex murmurs, "I've seen you angry... but never like this."

Adam stares at the burning Amibian dreadnoughts.

"I'm not angry."

His visor reflects the fire.

"I'm focused."

They find a fallen Knight transport.

Still smoking.

Still functional.

Its organic interior pulses faintly in the dark.

Jose steps back. "That thing looks alive."

Dex shrugs. "So are we. Let's ride."

Adam grips his rifle.

the Ark Starship turns its massive body toward Earth,

its engines glowing with eldritch light.

Evelyn's voice whispers again through Adam's helmet:

"Find me..."

The lunar horizon burns.

Adam rises slowly from the fallen pilot, dust settling around his boots in drifting, weightless spirals.

Something inside him cracks — not loudly, but like an old wound splitting open.

He closes his eyes...

...and the Moon dissolves away.

Adam is fourteen.

The world feels too loud. Too bright. Too heavy.

The TV glows in the dim apartment.

He sits at the kitchen table, homework spread out in messy piles, pencil tapping in a rhythm he can't control. Numbers blur. Words crawl. His chest tightens with frustration.

Then—

The front door slams open.

His father, David Warn, bursts into the apartment, laughing breathlessly as he kicks off his boots. He rushes over, grabs Adam's shoulders.

"Kiddo — did you see the protest on the news? They're listening. People are finally standing up!"

Adam smiles — small, shy, but real.

His father has that effect.

David ruffles his hair and drops into the seat beside him. "What're we working on?"

Adam pushes the worksheet toward him. "Math. I... I don't get it."

David leans in close, voice gentle. "Hey. Look at me."

Adam does.

"You can do anything," his father says softly. "Just put your mind to it."

The line becomes a promise — one Adam repeats to himself through every hardship of his young life.

David helps him with every problem.

He doesn't rush him.

Doesn't judge him.

Doesn't sigh in frustration.

He guides.

He encourages.

He loves.

Hours pass in peace.

Then—

A new broadcast interrupts the screen. Reporters shouting over gunfire. Smoke clouds. Screaming crowds.

And Adam sees it.

His father sees it too.

David's face goes pale.

That's his protest.

His movement.

His people.

Adam whispers, "Dad... don't go."

David kneels beside him, gripping his hands.

"I have to help them, or you will not live a safe life here in this City!."

Tears burn the back of Adam's eyes. "Please... please don't go."

His father hugs him — tight, warm, desperate.

"I'll be back. I promise."

Adam holds onto that promise like a lifeline.

But hours later—

The TV blares again.

News anchors stuttering.

Camera shaking.

A chaotic blur of bodies.

A gunshot.

A collapse.

A flash of David's jacket in the crowd.

Adam screams for him through the screen.

But the world doesn't listen.

Adam's eyes open.

The Moon is silent again.

The pilot's body lies still beside him.

Dex watches him carefully.

Jose lowers his head in respect.

Adam inhales — slow, controlled — the way his father taught him.

Dex puts a hand on his shoulder. "You good, brother?"

Adam nods once.

"I'm going to save her," he says. "No matter what's coming. No matter what it costs."

He looks up at the burning sky — at the Amibian army descending.

And for a moment...

He looks exactly like his father.

Strong.

Steady.

Unbreakable.

He whispers the words again, barely audible through the comms:

"You can do anything... just put your mind to it."

Jose and Dex exchange a look.

Raptor Squad rallies behind him.

And Adam steps into the war with renewed purpose.

they board the Amibian ship for the next battle.

Chapter 13

FALLING FROM GRACE

The alien craft pulses beneath their boots — alive, breathing, humming like a metallic heart. Organic plates stretch and contract along the walls as if inhaling them into its ribcage.

Dex grimaces. "I'm gonna be honest, this ship feels like the inside of a giant squid."

Jose taps the wall. It shudders. "Correction — a giant squid that hates us."

Adam steps into the pilot node — a throne of living wires and shifting geometrics. The seat shapes itself around him, tendrils curling gently up his spine.

He stiffens.

Dex frowns. "Adam...? You okay?"

Adam grips the armrests.

"Let's fly."

The ship responds to his intent instantly.

Lights flare.

Vessels detach.

Bio-reactors surge awake with a throbbing pulse.

Jose whistles. "Damn. You're good at this."

Adam's visor reflects alien glyphs racing across the interface. He doesn't blink.

"I want Earth," he says.

The ship interprets the command.

With a low, resonant roar, it blasts off the lunar surface, kicking up a plume of dust that ripples in slow-motion waves.

The sky collapses around them.

As they rise, the battlefield expands into a nightmare panorama:

Amibian dreadnoughts drift like skeletal titans

Human destroyers burn in silent firestorms

Escape pods fall like dying meteors

Orbital defense guns flicker and die

Plasma beams slice across the stars, carving glowing scars in the void.

A colossal Amibian carrier cracks open, spilling Knight-class soldiers into space, their swords shimmering with deep violet energy.

Dex leans forward. "They're everywhere—holy hell."

Jose checks his weapons rack. "Orbital is gone. They took out the whole ring."

Adam doesn't respond.

His jaw is tight.

Hands steady.

Eyes fixed on Earth's blue arc.

He feels Evelyn before her voice reaches him.

A faint whisper through the static:

"Adam..."

He freezes.

Dex turns. "Brother? You hearing her again?"

Adam nods slowly.

But something in his voice frightens even him.

"She's scared."

The ship jolts.

A swarm of Amibian interceptors locks onto them, approaching fast. Their wings buzz like angry insects.

Jose straps in. "Here we go! First wave incoming!"

Dex grins, adrenaline hitting. "Let's see what she can do, Adam!"

Adam spreads his palms along the pilot node.

"Fight," he commands.

The alien ship obeys instantly.

Organic wings unfold.

Tendrils retract.

Steering membranes stretch like a manta ray accelerating through water.

The ship spins into the swarm—

Laser fire streaks past.

Plasma arcs across the hull.

Adam dives, rolls, climbs—

They glide like something born in this battlefield.

Dex's sniper turret locks on. "Target painted."

He fires.

One interceptor erupts into silent flame, spinning away into the black.

Jose unloads dual cannons. "Who's next?! Let's dance!"

More enemies appear — dozens, then hundreds.

Adam growls.

"Hold on."

He pushes the ship into a nosedive so sudden Dex screams something in Japanese and Jose slams into his harness.

They thread between two dreadnought cannons as they fire, plasma beams barely missing the cockpit.

Dex pants. "Adam Warn, you madman—where did you learn that?!"

Adam's voice is dark. "Dad taught me to focus."

A beam slices past them.

Another shakes the ship.

Organic plating ripples, sealing instantly.

Jose gasps. "This thing heals itself?!"

Dex laughs. "Best stolen ride ever!"

Another wave hits.

Adam wills the ship to turn.

It obeys.

They break through the last line of interceptors and enter clear orbit.

Below them—

Earth burns.

City lights flicker out in massive patches.

Amibian dropships descend through the atmosphere like rain made of fire.

Explosions bloom across continents.

Jose's voice cracks. "God... we're losing."

Dex mutters, "Not while we're breathing."

Adam stares at the planet.

"Evelyn is down there," he whispers.

And then—

Her voice again.

More faint.

More corrupted.

More desperate.

"Adam... find me... please..."

His heart stops.

He grips the controls.

"I'm coming," he says. "I won't let him take you."

Dex places a hand on Adam's shoulder. "We got your back, brother."

Jose nods. "Always."

The moment hangs heavy.

The three of them breathing together.

United.

One heartbeat.

Adam angles the ship toward a burning section of the atmosphere.

The front viewport glows with re-entry fire.

He whispers one final promise:

"For her... for Earth... for all of us."

The alien ship dives—

Into flame.

Into war.

Into destiny.

The Ark Starship vibrates with a rising hum, like something vast beneath the hull is awakening. Dim red light pulses through the corridors as if the ship itself is breathing.

Victor Redmond stands before the main observation window, cloak billowing around him. His cybernetic eye blazes with streams of data fed directly into his cortex.

A flock of Amibian interceptors rushes past the viewport, their oily hulls reflecting the inferno of Earth's wounded atmosphere.

Victor's lips curl upward.

"He lives."

The central holographic sphere rotates beside him, projecting a swarm of trajectories. Amid the chaos, one signal burns brighter—

A stolen Amibian Knight transport.

Moving with unnatural precision.

Threading a needle through annihilation.

Victor zooms in.

Adam Warn.

Alive.

Defiant.

Charging into hell.

Victor laughs — softly at first, then sharper, edged with delight and fury.

"You stubborn bastard."

An officer approaches, six eyes blinking nervously. "My lord... our vessel... its pilot—"

"Is Adam," Victor finishes.

The officer swallows. "The probability of survival—"

"—is irrelevant," Victor snaps. "He is what I would have been if my world had not vomited me into the furnace."

Victor steps closer to the viewport.

The stolen ship streaks toward Earth like a single bright tooth in a jaw of darkness.

Victor whispers, "Come on, Adam. Fight me."

Another officer, this one heavily cybernetized, speaks cautiously. "What of Subject 07? Her readings deteriorate. Her mind—"

Victor's demeanor shifts.

He turns sharply.

"Bring her image up."

A hologram of Evelyn Lu materializes beside Adam's. She trembles inside the Tech-Mite harness on the Ark, her pupils flickering in a frantic cycle — dilating, shrinking, dilating again.

Her voice glitches through the chamber speakers:

"Ad...Am... f-f-find... me..."

Victor's cybernetic fingers curl with possessive anger.

"She calls for him. Even broken... even hollowing out... she resists."

His voice drops into a growl.

"Just like Jay."

He looks away quickly, as if the emotion disgusts him.

The Ark trembles — Nyarlathotep's presence brushing the edges of reality.

An ancient whisper threads through Victor's skull:

"He rises.

Break him.

Bring him."

Victor bows his head.

"Yes, Master. He comes to me by choice."

He looks back toward Earth, where Adam's ship blazes through the thermosphere.

A slow smile spreads across his face.

"You're ready," he whispers. "At last."

He places a hand on the glass, fingers spread.

"Do you know how long I've waited to kill the man I could have been?"

The viewport shudders as a new wave of Amibian reinforcements deploy.

Victor closes his eyes, savoring the taste of the coming battle.

"Welcome to the war, Adam Warn."

His eyelids lift, burning with orange light.

"Let's see who the universe chose correctly."

Chapter 14

CREATION OF ADAM

The Ark Starship groans around them like a living cathedral gone mad.

Raptor Squad advances down a spine of black metal, boots echoing against ribs of fused bone and plating. Glowing Amibian script pulses along the walls like veins, shivering in time with a distant, monstrous heartbeat.

Adam leads.

Dex covers the rear with his sniper rifle, eyes scanning for movement.

Jose walks in the middle, assault rifle raised, every muscle tense.

Above them, through occasional ruptures in the hull, Earth hangs in the void—bleeding light, burning at the edges where Amibian dropships rip through the atmosphere.

Jose murmurs, "Feels like walking down the throat of a god."

Dex replies, "Yeah, well, let's give it indigestion."

Adam doesn't answer.

His focus narrows to the waypoint on his HUD—

"The CORE!"

The origin of the annihilation beam that's already erased entire fleets and cities.

And somewhere inside this monster of a ship—

Evelyn.

Her voice still flickers at the edge of his thoughts like static on a dead channel.

Adam...

He tightens his grip on his sword hilt.

"We're close," he says. "Stay sharp."

They reach a door that isn't a door.

It's a membrane: black, wet, and pulsing, ringed by techno-organic metal. At its center, a circular emblem glows—the same pattern Evelyn traced absentmindedly once on a table, back when they were safe. Before all of this.

Dex shudders. "This thing better not blink at me."

Jose nods at Adam. "You're up, boss."

Adam steps forward. The membrane senses him, shivers, then splits open with a hiss, retracting into the walls like a living iris.

The chamber beyond is vast.

A bridge arcs out over an impossible abyss—an open chasm inside the ship, bottom swallowed by swirling light. The beam generator hangs from the ceiling like a black sun, its core a spinning ring of distortion that tears reality into a funnel of white and violet.

Lightning made of time and gravity lashes inward, feeding the singularity below.

Standing at the edge of that maelstrom, cloaked in shadow and orange light—

Victor Redmond.

And in front of him—bound in a lattice of Tech-Mite spine-cables, held up on her toes over nothing—

Evelyn.

Adam stops breathing.

Dex whispers, "Oh, no…"

Jose's voice breaks. "Eve…"

Victor turns.

His cloak sways with him, catching the light, his cybernetic eye burning like molten metal. When he smiles, it's like watching a scar open.

"Adam," he says. "You made it."

The voice hits Adam like a punch.

It's wrong.

It's twisted.

But beneath the metal, the distortion, the hate—

It's his own voice.

Adam forces the word out. "Victor."

Victor laughs softly. "We really should stop meeting like this. You in ruins. Me on top of them."

Dex mutters, "Okay, officially hate this guy."

Jose aims his rifle. "Let her go."

Victor doesn't even look at him.

He steps closer to Evelyn instead, placing a hand lightly against her cheek. The Tech-Mite cables tighten, making her gasp.

Her eyes meet Adam's across the chasm.

"Adam…" she whispers. "Don't…"

Victor leans close to her ear. "Say his name again like that, and he might actually jump."

Adam's heart hammers.

"Let. Her. Go."

Victor turns back toward him and spreads his arms slightly.

"Or what? You'll kill me? Tell me, Adam… what's it like to want to murder your own reflection?"

He steps farther into the light.

For the first time, Adam sees his face clearly.

Same jaw. Same bone structure. Same eyes—except Victor's are hard where Adam's are wounded.

And half of Victor's skull, shoulder, and chest are plated in intricate cybernetics, seamed with glowing veins.

Dex whispers, "Jesus… he really is you."

Victor nods once, almost theatrically. "Finally, someone gets it."

He gestures toward the beam.

"In my world, I died in the fire. In yours, you walked away. Different roll of the dice… different universe… different Adam."

His voice cools.

"I woke up inside Amibian machinery, rebuilt from ash and half a soul. I crawled through their wars. Lived in their cages. Watched Jay die screaming while your Earth… made peace. Unified. Pretended it learned something."

He snarls.

"You got Evelyn. I got a corpse and a god of chaos whispering in my ear."

He taps his temple.

"Tell me, Adam—why do you deserve this life more than I did?"

Adam steps onto the bridge.

His boots thud against the metal.

"Because I didn't sell my soul," he says. "You did."

Victor's smile is broken glass.

"Funny thing about souls. They don't do much against orbital bombardment and a mother who calls you a burden."

A crack ripples through Adam.

He hears his own memory in that word.

A door closing.

A suitcase dragging.

His mother's voice, trembling but cold—

"I can't do this anymore. He's too much. I'm too tired. I never get a break. Maybe... maybe he'd be better off without me."

Victor watches Adam's face and knows where his mind went.

"Oh. She said it there too, didn't she?" Victor asks softly. "We really were the same once."

He glances at Evelyn.

"Until the universe decided I was the broken one. The expendable Adam. The version who gets to be monstrous so you can feel heroic."

Adam's knuckles whiten on his sword.

Dex murmurs, "Don't listen to him, brother."

Jose lowers his rifle, hand drifting toward his mono-blade.

Victor spreads his arms.

"Here's how this goes," he says. "I turn on the beam fully. Every city that matters? Gone. Every timeline aligned to my will. Nyarlathotep gets his feast. I get... order."

He flicks a glance at Evelyn.

"And she stops being a liability."

He moves fast.

Too fast.

His cybernetic arm slams into Evelyn's restraints, unlocking them with a twitch of his fingers.

For half a second, she falls forward, toward the bridge.

Adam lunges.

Then Victor shoves her sideways—

off the edge—

into the churning white abyss.

"NO!" Adam roars.

He sprints.

Dex screams, "ADAM!"

Jose: "Don't—!"

Adam doesn't hear them.

He dives off the bridge.

The world rips open.

TURBO ignites on its own—

sensors overclocking, pain limits shattering, neural pathways burning.

Time slows.

The roar of the beam warps into a low groan. Evelyn falls in front of him—limbs weightless, hair floating upward, eyes wide and full of terror.

Adam pushes his body harder than it's ever gone. Every synapse in his brain screams. His vision tunnels, edges turning white.

He reaches for her.

His fingers brush her wrist.

Memories slam into him like bullets:

His father at the table, saying: You can do anything. Just put your mind to it.

His mother's back as she walks away.

Kids whispering about the "weird boy" who stares too long and talks too little.

The train impact. The moment everything changed.

Evelyn smiling at him over cheap coffee, saying, "You don't have to be anyone else to be enough."

The beam pulls harder.

TURBO pushes back.

His heart feels like it's going to burst.

He grabs her hand.

They spin together in the gravity storm, suit alarms screaming in his ears.

WARNING: TURBO DURATION EXCEEDED

NEURAL DAMAGE IMMINENT

Evelyn's voice cracks. "Adam! Let go—you'll die—"

"Not... happening," he grits.

He kicks off a piece of floating debris—someone's shattered armor, someone's last stand—and hurls both of them toward the collapsing bridge.

A piece of the Ark breaks free and collides with Evelyn, sending her trajectory sideways.

His grip slips.

Their fingers slide apart.

"ADAM!" she screams.

He slams into a jagged panel of ship debris, spine screaming, armor cracking. Evelyn spins away, drawn deeper into the light, into endless white.

Then—

She vanishes.

The beam swallows her whole.

TURBO shuts down like someone pulled a plug in his mind.

Pain slams in.

He lies there, gasping, chest on fire, limbs numb.

For a long second, he doesn't move.

The beam howls around him.

He realizes, with a coldness that hurts worse than his injuries:

He lost her.

Something inside Adam breaks. And something else wakes up.

He drags himself back onto the bridge, every motion a knife.

Dex rushes toward him. "Adam—Adam, talk to me—"

Adam shrugs him off gently but firmly.

His visor is cracked. One of his eyes glows a deeper blue now—almost black at the center, like it's staring into infinity.

Jose steps back, feeling something in the air change.

The entire Ark vibrates.

Victor stands near the core controls, watching, sword at his side.

He looks almost impressed.

"You jumped for her," Victor says. "I wondered if you'd really do it. You really are the better me."

He nods once, almost a bow.

"That's why you have to die."

Adam pulls his mono-blade.

When he speaks, his voice is calm.

"You first."

He lowers his head and whispers:

"ENGAGE FULL TURBO!!!"

The world fractures into shards of speed and clarity.

TURBO surges again, beyond safe limits. Every nerve in Adam's body ignites, telling him this is wrong, this is too far, this is where people die.

He doesn't care.

His eyes go dark blue, pupils shrunk to pinpoints.

Dex shouts something—

Jose reaches out—

The Ark tilts—

And Adam moves.

One moment, he's twenty meters away.

The next, he's in front of Victor, blade already swinging.

Victor barely brings his own sword up in time.

The clash rings like a bell across the chamber—

sparks exploding, energy flaring, metal wailing.

"You think you can kill me?" Victor snarls. "I survived things you can't imagine!"

They move in a blur—

strikes, parries, kicks, grapples—

two versions of the same man, one fueled by rage, the other by desperation and madness.

Victor's cybernetic arm catches Adam's swing and locks it in place. He leans close.

"We are the same."

Adam twists, slams his knee into Victor's chest.

"No," Adam says, teeth gritted. "I had someone who believed in me. You chose to be this."

Victor's eye flares.

He headbutts Adam, snapping his head back. "I chose to live. This is what surviving looks like when the universe spits you out!"

He slashes.

Adam dodges—barely—blade kissing his armor, carving a glowing line along his ribs.

Pain flares.

TURBO drowns it.

They circle.

Dex and Jose can only watch from the edge, weapons raised, unable to intervene without risking killing Adam.

"Come on, brother," Dex whispers. "End this."

Victor lunges again.

Adam doesn't step back this time.

He steps through the strike, taking the cut across his shoulder, ignoring the spray of blood that floats in slow arcs.

He rams his sword upward, locking Victor's arm aside, and drives his elbow into Victor's jaw.

Bone cracks.

Metal dents.

Victor staggers.

Adam presses the attack.

Each blow comes faster, sharper, more precise—

guided not just by training, but by something else:

All the years of feeling wrong.

Too quiet.

Too intense.

Too much.

All the days he wondered if his mother left because of him.

All the nights his father told him he wasn't broken.

All the loss. All the guilt. All the love.

He pours all of it into the blade.

Victor stumbles back toward the edge of the bridge.

"Look at you," Victor spits, laughing through blood. "You think this makes you a hero? You're just like me—you're breaking yourself for people who will never understand you."

Adam's eyes burn.

"Maybe," he says.

He raises his sword high.

"But I'd rather break for them than break them."

He triggers TURBO one last time.

The world stops.

Only he and Victor move.

Adam steps in, clean, sure, unstoppable.

The sword arcs—

Victor tries to raise his weapon.

Too slow.

The blade slices through Victor's neck in one perfect, savage stroke.

For a fraction of a second, Victor's head is still attached.

He meets Adam's eyes.

There's something like peace there.

"Finally," Victor whispers. "One of us... did it right."

Then his head separates from his body and drifts off, cloak billowing, blood beading into the air in a halo of red.

His body drops to its knees, then slowly topples, lifeless, into the abyss.

The Ark shudders.

The beam sputters.

Alarms scream.

PRIMARY CONTROL NODE LOST.

ANOMALOUS ENTITY AWAKENING.

Adam's sword hangs at his side.

Dex and Jose rush toward him.

"Adam!" Dex grabs his shoulders. "You did it! You—"

He stops.

Adam is swaying.

His eyes flicker.

HUD glitching.

Suit trembling.

Jose sees it first.

"His neck port," Jose says, voice tight. "Look."

A faint, metallic shape crawls at the base of Adam's skull—

small, spiderlike, half-phased into the neural link.

A Tech-Mite.

It twitches once.

Syncs.

Latches on.

Adam's breath stutters.

For a heartbeat, he hears three voices in his head:

His father—

You can do anything, just put your mind to it.

His mother—

He's too much. I can't handle him.

And something new.

Deep.

Cosmic.

Hungry.

"Good," Nyarlathotep whispers. "Now we can begin."

Chapter 15

FALL FAR FROM THE TREE

Victor's head hits the metal floor with a muted, echoing thud.

The body — headless, sparking, twitching — collapses to its knees and folds forward like a puppet cut from its strings. The sword in Adam's hands drips with burning violet oil and shattered circuits.

Silence swallows the chamber.

Then Adam's knees give out.

He drops beside Victor's corpse, chest heaving, lungs clawing for air. His vision fractures into shards — orange light, blue fire, flickers of Evelyn falling, falling, falling—

His pulse slams against his skull.

TOO MUCH TURBO.

Neurological overload.

Brainstem destabilizing.

His HUD screams warnings, but Adam barely hears them.

He hears only Evelyn.

Not her voice.

Not her real one.

A ghost of it.

A glitching whisper.

"...Adam... come... find..."

It slices through him.

He grips the floor.

"No... no, stay with me—stay with me—"

His words smear.

Sound bends.

Gravity shifts sideways.

He reaches for the ledge where she fell.

He sees nothing but swirling blackness — a writhing void of fractured spacetime from the Ark's unfinished beam core.

His throat closes.

"I'm sorry... Evelyn..."

Dex's voice erupts from behind him, desperate:

"ADAM! Brother—HEY—don't you do this!"

Adam turns —

And sees Dex and Jose rushing toward him.

But their faces warp.

Dex's outline splits in two, blurry, like a double exposure. Jose's visor flickers, but Adam sees another face overlaid on his — something pale, eyeless, smiling too wide.

Adam gasps. "No... not you too..."

Jose kneels beside him immediately. "Adam—listen to me—your suit's burning you alive from the inside, we need to shut TURBO down—"

Adam jerks back violently.

"No! If I stop... she dies. I CAN'T STOP—"

Dex grabs him. "Adam! She's already gone—"

Adam slams a fist into Dex's chestplate hard enough to dent it.

Dex flies back several feet.

"DON'T SAY THAT!" Adam roars.

His voice is deeper.

Harsher.

Layered with something not his.

Jose stumbles back, raising both hands. "Adam... stay with me. Look at me—LOOK at me."

But Adam's pupils dilate past human limits.

His breath becomes ragged like an animal.

Something crawls beneath the skin of his neck — a faint metallic ripple that wasn't there before.

Dex speaks through a strained wheeze, trying to stand again. "Jose... it's the Tech-Mite... the suit's letting it in—"

Jose freezes. "No. No no no—Adam—just breathe. Please."

Adam clutches the side of his helmet, trembling.

"Something's in my head..."

His voice cracks.

Breaks.

"My... mom."

Dex stiffens. "Adam—"

Adam's throat trembles like a child trying not to cry.

"She... she left me because I was different... wrong... and I hear her voice again—"

A whisper slithers through the room.

Not from speakers.

Not from the air.

From inside Adam.

"Wrong child. Broken boy."

Adam screams.

The sound is raw — primal — torn out of him like something being ripped from bone.

Dex's eyes widen. "That's not him. That's it. The Tech-Mite."

Jose moves fast.

He grabs Adam's helmet with both hands. "Adam! Look at me—NOT at what you're hearing. Adam—listen—your father loved you—"

Another whisper coils inside Adam's skull:

"Lies... your father died because of you..."

Adam convulses.

His visor flickers between blue and an unnatural orange.

Dex draws his blade. "Jose—get back—he's losing control!"

Jose doesn't move. "No. I'm not leaving him."

Adam's breathing becomes unnatural — a stuttering gasp, almost insect-like.

He whispers:

"I couldn't save her...

I couldn't save my dad...

I couldn't save Evelyn..."

Jose leans in closer. "Adam. Brother. You aren't supposed to. That's not how love works."

Dex tightens his grip on his blade. "Jose—"

Jose cuts him off. "Not yet."

Adam's fingers dig into the floor so hard the metal bends.

His voice fractures into two tones:

"My father said...

I could do anything...

Just put my mind to it..."

His eyes snap toward Dex and Jose — glowing with a luminous, unnatural midnight blue.

"But what if my mind isn't mine anymore?"

A long silence.

Then—

Jose whispers, broken:

"Oh God... Adam..."

Dex steps forward finally.

"Adam... we're gonna help you. But right now? We gotta MOVE. The Ark's collapsing. And something out there is waking up."

Adam sways violently.

And then—

His posture shifts.

His muscles coil.

His visor darkens to near black.

When he speaks, the voice is layered with something cosmic:

"Nyarlathotep is waiting."

Dex's entire body goes cold.

Jose stumbles backward.

Adam stands.

Slowly.

Like a puppet rising.

The Tech-Mite corruption has begun.

And the universe holds its breath.

The corridor twists again.

Metal folds like a muscle contracting, the Ark shifting its internal geometry to confuse him. Adam grips the wall to steady himself—then recoils.

It moves under his touch.

Veins pulse beneath the alien plating.

A whisper ripples through the air.

"Do not run from what you are becoming..."

Adam shudders violently.

"Shut up," he mutters, pushing forward.

But the voice follows.

A second whisper joins the first—feminine, familiar, frightened.

"Adam... please... hurry..."

Evelyn.

He freezes.

"Evelyn! Evelyn, where are you?!"

Her voice glitches.

Fragments.

Echoes.

Like a broken radio signal smashed together with screams.

"Ad—am—don't—come—he—he—he sees you—"

Static tears her voice apart.

Adam sprints.

The ship reacts—walls peel back, corridors elongate, lights dim into violet darkness. The Ark wants him to run, as if pulling him toward the deepest part of itself.

Through the shifting dark, he catches his reflection in a splitting metal panel—

His visor flickers.

For half a second, he sees:

Eyes glowing deep blue, pulsing like Tech-Mite nodes

Veins along his neck lit faintly under the skin

A crawling shadow across the side of his helmet

Adam staggers back.

"No—no, no—this isn't me."

But the truth crushes him:

The Tech-Mite residue from Evelyn... got into his suit.

Got into him.

He squeezes his head between trembling hands as another pulse hits him—like cold needles sliding inside his skull.

He clenches his teeth. "Fight it. Fight it."

A memory slams into him—

David Warn kneels beside him at the kitchen table.

"Adam... listen. Sometimes your mind tries to trip you. It doesn't mean you're broken. It means you're stronger than the noise."

Adam breathes, shaking.

His father rests a hand on his cheek.

"And I will always be proud of you, son. No matter how the world tries to twist you."

The vision snaps.

He wakes up holding Jose in the Beam, obliterating every cell in his body.

Dex watches in fear as well as hopelessness.

But he does not give up on his brother, Dex rushes his mono blade through Adam's shoulder pinning him to the ship.

Dex removes the Tech-Mite with his bare hands from his neck, as blood and skin crushes in his palm along with Victor's horrid creation.

Adam was freed of corruption.

Dex and Adam hugged Mourning Jose and collecting themselves as much as they could.

and then.

Footsteps echo behind them.

They rise, turning with a snarl—rifle up—

But it isn't a soldier.

It's a Knight.

A towering blue-armored Amibian Knight steps out from the shadows, four arms raised, blade humming with cosmic vibration.

It freezes.

Then kneels.

Lowering its head in submission.

Adam steps back. "Wait... what the hell?"

The Knight speaks through a translator node embedded in its throat.

A deep, resonant voice.

"You carry the scent of corruption.

The Ark recognizes you.

You are becoming... favored."

Adam grips his rifle tighter.

"Where is Evelyn Lu?"

The Knight tilts its head.

"Subject Seven is in the Sanctum Core."

Adam's pulse spikes. "Take me there."

The Knight rises.

"As you command."

Adam blinks hard.

and he forces himself forward.

He must get to her.

Chapter 16

THE KING AND THE PAWN

Silence doesn't exist in the Void.

Not here.

Not in this place between stars, where the laws of reality peel away like old paint. The air—if this dimension has such a thing—vibrates with whispers that aren't sound but pressure: a weight pressing against the skull from the inside.

They Stood at the gate to the void where the Knight watched them in Curiosity.

Adam moves forward, boots landing on a surface that isn't ground but a solid shadow—ripples of light shivering beneath every step. Dex stays behind him, breathing hard, rifle tracking the empty dark.

If it can even be called empty.

Shapes flicker in the distance: impossible silhouettes, elongated and twisted, walking with too many joints. Some crawl. Some float. Some pulse like organs suspended in glass.

None of them come close.

They watch.

They wait.

The Void knows who has entered it.

Dex swallows. "I hate this place. Everything feels... wrong."

Adam doesn't answer.

His eyes glow faint blue, pulsing faintly with something that isn't his own making. He's still riding the edges of Full TURBO—his nerves raw, skin buzzing, thoughts sharp enough to cut him from the inside, is in other words called Turbo Eyes.

The God's Voice inside his skull scratches faintly.

Not yet taking control.

But hungry.

Dex notices the tremor in Adam's hands. "You need to slow down. You push again like you did back on the Ark... it'll fry your brain."

Adam's voice sounds distant. "I can't slow down."

A whisper slides through the Void—Evelyn's voice, cracked down the middle like a broken bell:

"Adam..."

He stops.

Head tilts.

Chest tightens.

Breath trembles.

Dex steps closer. "Talk to me, brother. What do you hear?"

Adam's jaw clenches. "Her."

Another whisper.

Soft.

Unsteady.

Dying.

"Adam... hurry..."

He turns his head upward.

Above them hangs a tear in reality—an enormous wound in the Void's fabric. It hangs like a vertical ocean, colors bleeding in and out:

violet, black, silver, the deep red of dying stars. Tendrils of shadow curl from its edges like the fingers of a sleeping god.

Evelyn is somewhere beyond it.

Lost.

Trapped.

Held between worlds by a cosmic hand older than galaxies.

Dex looks up and exhales sharply. "We're really doing this. We're actually going into that thing."

Adam takes another step toward the rift.

The shadows nearest them recoil, hissing softly.

The Void reacts to him—its fabric bending at the edges of his presence.

Dex rests a hand on his shoulder. "Adam. Before we go any farther... I gotta know you're still you. The Voices inside you, the TURBO overuse—this place could tip you over."

Adam doesn't look at him.

"Dex... I know."

"Do you?"

Adam finally turns.

And Dex sees it—the truth behind Adam's eyes.

Not madness.

Not corruption.

Not Nyarlathotep's influence.

Fight.

Pain.

Resolve.

And beneath it all...

That unmistakable stillness.

That deep-focus calm that Adam always had.

The same calm he used when the world overwhelmed him.

The same calm he used when crowds were too loud.

The same calm that made him stand alone on the train tracks that day, frozen between panic and fate.

His father's voice echoes in his head.

"You can do anything, son.

Just put your mind to it."

Adam closes his eyes.

He breathes once.

Deep. Steady.

And the tremor in his hands stops.

When he opens them again, the blue glow steadies.

"I'm here," he tells Dex. "I'm still here."

Dex nods, swallowing emotion. "Then let's go get Evelyn back."

He lifts his rifle.

Adam raises his sword.

The rift pulses—throbbing like the heartbeat of a star.

Another whisper echoes from within:

"Come to me."

But this voice is not Evelyn's.

Not human.

Not mortal.

It crawls along bone and nerve like cold fire.

Nyarlathotep knows they've entered his realm.

Dex mutters, "We are so screwed."

Adam steps forward.

"No," he whispers. "We're not."

He grips the mono-blade tighter.

"Not until the god bleeds."

The Void shifts.

The rift yawns wider.

And two silhouettes—two soldiers, broken but unbowed—walk into the wound between worlds.

Ready to face the crawling chaos itself.

Chapter 17

THE CHAIR

The tear in reality opens with a sound Adam cannot name — not thunder, not metal, not flesh — something older, deeper, something that hums inside bone marrow.

He stands at the edge of it.

Purple-black light spirals inward, folding space like a collapsing throat. The dimensional key vibrates in his hand, glowing with the last remnant of Victor's stolen life-force.

Dex limps beside him, armor scorched, shoulder bleeding through shattered plates.

"Adam..." Dex breathes, staring into the tear. "This is suicide."

Adam doesn't answer.

Because Evelyn's scream still echoes through him — the moment she slipped away, the moment Victor pushed her into the abyss, the moment Adam jumped and failed to reach her.

He hears it again now.

Eve... Eve... I'm coming...

But another voice answers.

"WELCOME..."

A whisper like a thousand throats speaking at once.

Dex swallows hard. "That's not her."

Adam steps forward.

"No. That's what took her."

The tear widens.

Gravity bends backward, forward, sideways. The air warps. Dust and debris spiral upward into the darkness as if the void is inhaling.

Dex grips Adam's arm. "Brother... please. You're not stable. That Tech-Mite is was in your suit. You're hearing things—"

Adam's head snaps toward him, eyes glowing faint sapphire and darkening around the edges.

"I'm in control, its not in me anymore!"

Dex's expression tightens. "You say that... but you don't look like Adam right now."

Adam breathes in slowly.

He remembers his father's voice.

You can do anything... just put your mind to it.

A promise. A lifeline.

He steadies.

"Evelyn is in there," he says. "And I won't lose her again."

Dex stares into the swirling abyss — a churning ocean of stars, blood, and impossible geometries.

"You saved my life," Dex whispers. "Jose saved mine. I'm not letting you go alone."

Adam turns toward him fully.

"You're hurt."

Dex smirks faintly. "Hurting means I'm alive."

A violent ripple shudders through the tear, the darkness inside it blooming outward like a monstrous flower.

Adam grips Dex's shoulder.

"I'm glad you're here."

Dex nods once. "Raptor Squad. Till the end."

They step forward together.

The void swallows them whole.

The realm is not darkness. It is depth.

Space folds inward until direction stops existing. Adam feels his boots touch a surface — but the surface feels alive, like the skin of a titan. Stars pulse beneath it. Rivers of shifting symbols flow through cracks.

Dex stumbles, clutching his ribs. "What... what is this place?"

Adam looks around.

The "sky" is a tapestry of cathedrals made from bone and stardust. Each structure floats inverted, held by nothing, suspended in the breath of a sleeping god.

And then Adam sees it.

Floating above the landscape—

A swirling monolith of tendrils and spines.

Eyes — thousands — blooming open across its surface.

Teeth growing along its limbs like evolving constellations.

A creature the size of a city.

A presence older than worlds.

Nyarlathotep.

The God Below Stars.

The Devourer of Dimensions.

Its voice slides into their minds like ice water.

"SO... YOU COME IN FLESH."

Dex falls to one knee, clutching his head. "Get... out... of me—"

Adam grabs him, pulling him upright.

The god's shadow expands, flooding the valley of broken stars.

"YOU ARE CRACKED, LITTLE ADAM."

"YOUR MIND IS OPEN."

"COME CLOSER..."

Adam grits his teeth. The God's voice pulses in his neural port, sending a shockwave down his spine.

His vision splits.

One side shows Evelyn's fall.

The other shows his mother walking away from him.

Both are lies.

Both are attacks.

He whispers to himself: "This is not real. Focus."

Nyarlathotep's form shifts, bending into the shape of Victor for a moment — burned, broken, headless — mocking Adam's guilt.

Dex draws his sword, hands trembling. "Adam... that thing... it's inside our thoughts—"

Adam steps forward.

"No. It's trying to be."

The god's laughter ripples through the void, cracking space like glass.

"YOU WILL JOIN ME.

JUST AS THE OTHER YOU DID."

Adam freezes.

Dex does too.

"What...?" Dex whispers.

Nyarlathotep's tendrils twist, showing a vision:

Victor kneeling before the cosmic god, surrendering his soul, eyes torn out and replaced by orange fire.

The god whispers:

"HE BEGGED ME TO MAKE HIM STRONG."

Adam's heart feels like it's being crushed.

Victor wasn't born a monster.

He was broken into one.

Nyarlathotep's voice hammers him again:

"HE WAS A BETTER VERSION OF YOU."

Adam's fists shake.

"No."

"YOU ARE WEAK WHERE HE WAS STRONG."

"No."

"YOU COULD NOT SAVE YOUR FATHER."

Adam staggers.

Dex grabs him. "Adam! Stay with me!"

"YOU COULD NOT SAVE EVELYN."

Adam roars — a primal, anguished sound that shakes the entire realm.

The Turbo Eyes awakens inside him.

Blue circuits burn across his armor. His eyes go flame-sapphire, then darken toward black. Power radiates from him, cracking the surface beneath his feet.

Dex stumbles back. "Brother—! Fight it!"

Adam drops to one knee, clawing at his helmet. "Not... now... please..."

Nyarlathotep extends a tendril the size of a building.

"YES. LET IT IN."

"COME TO ME."

Adam screams.

And then—

A hand touches his shoulder.

Warm.

Soft.

Human.

A whisper — faint but unmistakable:

"Adam..."

He freezes.

He knows that voice.

"Evelyn...?"

Her voice drifts like a fading star.

"Keep fighting... please..."

Adam forces a breath.

And another.

And another.

Dex kneels beside him, gripping his arm.

"Come on, brother. You're stronger than him."

Adam looks into the abyss of Nyarlathotep's thousand eyes.

His voice steadies.

"I am Adam Warn. Son of David Warn. Raptor Squad. And I am not yours."

The Tech-Mite flickers — confused.

Then dims.

Adam rises.

Nyarlathotep recoils slightly, as if insulted that something so small dares defy him.

"THEN DIE IN PIECES."

The god's entire body shifts, preparing to strike.

Dex draws his sword. "Adam...?"

Adam steps forward.

"We're not dying today."

He grips his blade.

"And we're not leaving without her."

The void begins to collapse inward.

Nyarlathotep descends like a falling mountain.

Adam charges.

Dex screams and charges beside him.

And the war between man and cosmic god begins.

Adam tore through the shattered corridors of Nyarlathotep's palace, moving in **zero gravity**, boots kicking off broken walls and floating debris as he cut his way forward. The structure itself seemed alive—angles folding in on themselves, impossible geometry clawing at his senses. Every slash of his blade carved through reality as much as flesh, yet still **Nyarlathotep loomed**, vast and mocking, a god wearing a thousand lies.

The cosmic demon pressed harder, warping space around Adam, forcing him to bear more terror than any human should. Still, Adam fought on—because Evelyn was somewhere in this nightmare, and that truth outweighed fear.

Dex's Discovery

Elsewhere in the palace, Dex moved like a ghost.

He slipped through shadowed chambers, bypassing eldritch sentries and warped corridors, following a faint resonance—the hum of something *wrong*. It led him to a sealed prison chamber wrapped in dimensional locks.

Inside, suspended in restraints of living energy, was Evelyn.

"Found you," Dex whispered.

Without hesitation, he planted charges and blew the locks apart, the chamber screaming as reality snapped back into place. Evelyn collapsed forward, free at last.

The palace shook violently as Adam clashed with Nyarlathotep again, the god's form fracturing and reforming with every blow.

Dex's voice cut through the chaos.

"ADAM!" he shouted over the comms, panic and urgency bleeding together.

"The Dimensional Key—throw it!"

Adam didn't hesitate.

He hurled the Key through the void, spinning end over end until Dex caught it clean.

In the same instant, Dex shoved Evelyn forward, throwing her directly into Adam's arms as the god roared in fury.

"Go," Dex said—his voice steady, but his eyes afraid. "Save yourselves."

Adam stared at him, horror dawning. "You were my brother."

Dex gave a tight smile, pain and resolve mixing in his expression. "And you will always be mine," he said. "Now I need to give Jose the last laugh... now go."

Sacrifice

Adam and Evelyn ran—weightless, desperate—toward the Void Gate as Dex turned back toward annihilation.

With shaking hands, Dex overloaded the Dimensional Key, pushing it beyond its limits, pressing it into his TURBO-CORE on his Suit, funneling every ounce of Turbo energy into its core. Space collapsed inward as the Key detonated—a star born inside the Void, an atomic cataclysm that tore Nyarlathotep from existence.

The Void sealed shut.

Not just closed—but locked forever.

Nyarlathotep would never touch this dimension again. Or any other.

Dex died in that final, blinding light.

Adam and Evelyn were thrown clear, tumbling into safety as silence reclaimed the universe.

For a moment, neither spoke.

Then Adam pulled Evelyn close and kissed her—not knowing if it was their first true moment of peace... or their last.

His voice broke as reality set in.

"I needed better for them," Adam said quietly.
"They shouldn't have died."

Evelyn reached up, running her fingers through his hair—slow, grounding, full of love and grief.

"They were great men," she said softly.
"And you have something no god can take from you."

Adam looked at her.

"The memories," Evelyn continued.
"You'll always have the good ones."

Chapter 18

ASHES AND HORIZONS

The sky over Earth is wrong.

What used to be a clean blue dome is streaked with faint, fading scars—burnt contrails from ships that never came home, ion trails from Amibian engines, aurora-like ripples where Nyarlathotep's presence once pressed against the atmosphere.

Adam watches it through the reinforced window of the recovery ward.

From here, LightBridge City looks fractured but alive. Sections still burn. Towers are half missing. But lights are on again. Drones crawl across damaged roads. Evac shuttles ferry survivors between districts, like white blood cells trying to patch a wounded body.

His reflection stares back at him in the glass.

Helmet off.

Hair longer. Messier.

Eyes that used to be simply tired now carry something else.

He lifts a hand and touches the faint scar at his temple—where the Tech-Mite tried to nest, where Nyarlathotep tried to climb into his thoughts.

It didn't get everything.

Didn't get him.

A soft knock comes from the door behind him.

"You going to brood there all day," Evelyn says, "or are you going to let me in?"

Adam turns.

She's leaning against the doorway, NEO-MED bandage still wrapped around her ribs, hair tied back in a messy knot. There's a thin, pale line on her neck where the harness once sat, where the god and the parasite used her as a conduit.

She smiles anyway.

It's small and tired.

But it's hers.

"I thought I left the door unlocked," Adam says.

"You did." She limps in, making a show of exaggerated effort. "I just wanted to see whether you'd tell me to go away."

"I wouldn't."

"Yeah," she murmurs. "I know."

She steps up beside him, following his gaze out the window.

They stand there in silence for a while.

Down below, a section of LightBridge flickers—whole blocks going dark, then sputtering back on. Emergency grid rerouting. People cheering faintly when the lights return.

"Looks like a broken circuit board," Evelyn says.

"Looks like home trying to reboot," Adam answers.

She nudges his shoulder with hers. "You always think in tech metaphors?"

"Mostly in patterns," he says quietly. "Lines. Loops. Things that repeat."

She studies him for a moment. "You're talking about more than the skyline."

He doesn't look away from the window.

"Nyarlathotep thought it could... use that. The way my brain works. The way I see things. It pushed its voice into every crack. Every pattern. Tried to fill the spaces."

"You fought it," she says. "You won."

"Only because of what my dad said. Only because I grabbed onto that and refused to let go." His jaw tightens. "It used the same words my mother did when she left. The same tone. The shame. The 'you're too much' and 'you're too strange' and 'why can't you just be normal'... It wanted me to drown in that."

Evelyn's voice softens. "But you didn't."

"No." He finally looks at her. "Because it was wrong. I'm not broken. My mind isn't a defect to exploit. It's the reason I saw the cracks in the god's tricks. The loops. The tells. The way its threats repeated with different skins." He swallows. "I didn't beat it in spite of being autistic."

He says the word like it's a blade he's finally learned how to hold without cutting himself.

"I beat it because I am."

Evelyn's eyes glisten, but she doesn't look away.

"I know," she says. "I kind of figured it out a while ago."

"You did?"

She laughs softly. "Adam, you sort things into patterns when you're stressed. You rehearse conversations in your head three times before you talk. You hyperfocus on tactical layouts like they're puzzles you can't put down. And—this is the big one—you flinch when people change plans on you mid-mission."

He winces. "That obvious?"

"To me?" She nods. "Yeah. But none of that ever made you less." Her voice goes firm. "It's part of how you see the world. How you noticed things the rest of us missed. How you read the battlefield. How you saved me."

He looks down.

She reaches for his hand.

"You are not broken," she says. "You're the reason we're still here."

He squeezes her fingers.

"Dex isn't," he says quietly. "Jose isn't."

Her smile falters.

The room seems smaller suddenly, like the walls lean in to listen.

"Yeah," she whispers. "I know."

The memorial platform is built out of salvaged metal and shattered glass.

It sits on a terrace overlooking the battered river that snakes through LightBridge City. The water is murky, choked with debris, but the current still moves. The world refuses to stop.

Flags—Earth's, allied nations, Amibian rogue factions who turned against Nyarlathotep—hang in ragged lines overhead. Names scroll in holographic panels along the far wall, an endless list of the dead.

Kelsey Reyes.

John Wolfgrove.

Jose Fuentes.

Dexter Yoi.

Adam stands with Evelyn among a crowd of soldiers, technicians, medics, civilians in mismatched clothes. Turbo-Trooper armor gleams here and there, patched and scorched. Many suits stand empty, helmets resting on folded flags.

General Osei speaks at a podium, voice amplified over the courtyard.

"...and to those who fought in the dark while the rest of us saw only the dawn, we say: we remember. There is no future without the blood you gave."

Adam barely hears her.

The words wash over him, blurred.

He stares at the holographic line where Jose's name hangs, bright and sharp, next to Dex's. His mind flashes through images: Jose's smirk. The way he moved silently through enemy lines. Dex's stupid jokes. Dex's hand on his shoulder before the jump into Nyarlathotep's void.

Top squad, Raptor Squad.

He hears Dex laughing it like a punchline, and Jose's Inspiring words.

A quiet force settles beside him.

Osei's old dress cap is clutched in Evelyn's hand. She never knew the Commander the way Adam did, but she holds it carefully, reverently, like something sacred.

"You want to say something?" she asks.

Adam shakes his head. "I don't do speeches."

"You already did one," she says. "When you refused to let that... thing take your mind. When you chose to keep going even after Dex and Jose..."

His throat closes.

He manages, "I failed them."

"No." Her voice is sharp. "You didn't."

"I killed Jose," he says. There's no flinching away from it now. No softening. "The Tech-Mite used me as a weapon and I still swung. I was in there. I saw it. I felt—"

"You fought," she says. "You fought like hell. And Dex knew that. He saw who you were. That's why he trusted you, even at the end. That's why he died giving you the chance to finish it."

Adam's hands shake.

Evelyn shifts closer, shoulder against his.

"Do you honestly think he'd want you standing here thinking you're a failure?" she asks. "Because I know what he'd say."

Adam snorts bitterly. "Oh yeah? What's that?"

She drops her voice into a rough Dex impression.

"'Top squad doesn't mope, Warn. Top squad gets back up and pisses in the god of chaos' coffee.'"

Adam chokes on a laugh that hurts his lungs.

"I can hear him saying that," he whispers.

"Then hold onto that," she says gently. "Not the moment you lost him. The reasons he stood beside you at all."

The General calls for a moment of silence.

Everyone bows their heads.

Adam closes his eyes.

In the dark behind his eyelids, he doesn't see Nyarlathotep.

Doesn't see Victor's blade.

Doesn't see the Tech-Mite crawling through his neural pathways.

He sees his father at the kitchen table.

You can do anything. Just put your mind to it.

He sees Jose laughing as he vaults a barricade during training.

He sees Dex in the Ark's void, flicking off the Cosmic God.

He sees Evelyn, suspended between worlds, and the way her fingers felt when they finally closed around his again after the fight.

He doesn't recite a prayer.

He just says, thank you.

And hopes the dead can hear it.

After the ceremony, the crowd disperses slowly—families clustering around names, soldiers embracing, medics standing alone at the back, not sure which version of hell they're supposed to grieve first.

Adam and Evelyn walk down the steps together.

A man in a crisp uniform intercepts them.

Gray hair. Lined face. Eyes like worn steel.

"Trooper Warn," he says. "and Lady Lu."

Adam straightens instinctively. "Sir."

The man nods once. "At ease. I'm not here to drag you into another fight. Not today."

"Then you're already my favorite officer," Dex would've said.

Adam bites back the ghost of the line.

The man continues, "The Turbo-Trooper program is being... reassessed. After everything that's happened—the Tech-Mites, the Amibian infiltration, Nyarlathotep—there are some who want it shut down completely."

Evelyn's jaw tightens. "They think we're a liability."

"They think you're weapons," the man says. "And weapons make politicians nervous when they've seen what those weapons can do."

He studies Adam's face.

"I've read the reports," he says. "All of them. Including what happened when the Tech-Mite took hold."

Adam looks away.

The officer's tone softens.

"Most soldiers break when something gets inside their head. You broke a god instead."

"Not alone," Adam says quietly.

"Yes," the man nods. "With your team. What's left of it."

He glances between Adam and Evelyn.

"We can't pretend this war didn't change the board. Humanity isn't alone anymore. The Amibian aren't either—some of their factions are already negotiating terms. Ulrakk's people claim this was never their will."

Evelyn nods. "Because it wasn't. Nyarlathotep turned them into cattle for its own hunger."

"The point is," the man says, "the world is going to need people who can operate in the gray. Between dimensions. Between species. Between... realities."

He steps back, gives them space.

"You two are at the center of that whether you like it or not. I'm not asking for an answer today. Just know this: if you want to walk away, you've earned it. If you want to build something better than what Reyes and Wolfgrove were handed... we'll back you. Carefully. Quietly."

Adam studies him.

"What would it look like?" he asks. "This new thing."

"Not Turbo-Troopers," the man says. "Not like before. Less blind obedience, more... informed consent." His eyes flicker with wry humor. "Fewer unknown alien artifacts fused directly to the brain, too."

Evelyn smirks. "That's good. Because I'm not letting anyone near his head again."

Adam glances at her.

The officer nods. "Think on it. There's time. For once, we're not seconds from annihilation."

He leaves them with a brief salute.

They watch him go.

Evelyn exhales. "You believe him?"

Adam looks out toward the river, where kids play along the cracked embankment under the watchful eyes of armored soldiers.

"I believe we're still here," he says. "That's new."

She bumps his shoulder. "You think you could handle not being shot at for five minutes?"

He actually smiles.

"I could try," he says. "Might need you to remind me I don't have to run toward every explosion anymore."

"Deal," she says. "But you know it's you and me versus whatever comes next, right? Whether that's paperwork... or another cosmic horror."

He nods.

"Yeah," he says. "I know."

They stand there at the edge of the terrace, watching the city try to remember how to be a home instead of a battlefield.

The scars in the sky are still there.

So are the lights below.

For the first time in a long time, Adam lets himself feel both at once without flinching.

Later, alone again in the ward, he sits on the edge of the bed and pulls up the personal log Reyes forced every trooper to keep.

"You'll want a record," she'd said. "Even if you don't think so now. Especially if you don't think so."

He scrolls past old entries—brief, clinical, stiff. Mission times. Kill counts. Tactical notes.

He opens a new one.

The cursor blinks.

He takes a breath.

LOG ENTRY 001: NOT A MISSION REPORT

Name: Adam Warn

Status: Alive (somehow)

Condition: Tired. Grateful. Still figuring it out.

Notes:

I used to think there was something wrong with me. That the way my mind works was a flaw that made everything harder—for me and for everyone around me.

A god tried to use that.

Tried to turn it into chains.

It failed.

I see patterns. I hold onto words. I lock onto promises and don't let go. That's not a curse. That's who I am. That's how I fought back.

Dex and Jose are gone. Reyes and Wolfgrove too. But I'm still here. Evelyn is still here. The world is damaged, not destroyed.

For the first time, "still here" feels like more than survival.

It feels like a beginning.

He pauses.

Then adds one last line.

Dad was right.

You can do anything. Just put your mind to it.

He saves the entry.

Outside, the sky doesn't magically heal. The scars don't vanish.

But dawn still shows up anyway.

And for the first time, Adam lets himself imagine there might be a future that isn't just war.

Epilogue

"EVERYTHING HAPPENS FOR A REASON"

1 **month later.....**

A soft hand touches his.

He turns—and there she is.

Evelyn.

Alive. Whole. Breathing.

Her hair falls over her shoulders like gold caught in morning light. Her eyes—clear again, free of the parasite's shimmer—fill with tears the moment she sees him awake.

"You scared me," she whispers.

Adam's throat tightens. "You scared me first."

She laughs, choked, and collapses into his arms. He holds her the way a drowning man clutches the surface—tight, desperate, grateful.

He feels the warmth of her heartbeat under his palm.

Proof.

A miracle.

The door opens.

General stands there—alive, patched together by every medical miracle the Antarctic base can spare. Her arm is in a sling, her side wrapped, but her voice is steady.

"You two have people waiting," she says.

Adam can see the weight she carries—the losses, the scars—but behind it, pride.

A soldier's pride.

When she closes the door, Evelyn pulls back just enough to look into Adam's eyes.

"What happens now?" she asks.

Adam answers without hesitation:

"Now... we live."

Snow whips against the ice cliffs as wind howls across the remote outpost. Inside the chapel—small, warm, lit by soft lamps—Adam stands in a simple black uniform, hands trembling just enough to give him away.

Dex's dog tags hang around his neck.

Jose's insignia is pinned to his chest.

Raptor Squad is smaller now—but not gone.

Evelyn enters in a white coat trimmed with silver, her hair braided with blue ribbon from her old flight jacket. She walks toward Adam with a smile that breaks him open from the inside.

Chaplin officiates.

"This war isn't over," he says, voice steady. "But today... we take something back."

Adam and Evelyn speak their vows quietly, intimately, as the storm rattles the glass.

When Adam kisses her—slow, gentle, unhurried—it feels like the first warmth after a lifetime of cold.

The chapel erupts into applause from the surviving squad members, scientists, and medics. Someone cries. Someone whistles. Someone shouts Dex's old line:

"Raptor Squad forever!"

Adam laughs into Evelyn's hair.

"Forever," he whispers.

LATER — ALONE ON THE ICE

The night sky glows with auroras streaking green and violet across the heavens. Adam stands on the observation deck, Evelyn's hand intertwined with his.

For a moment, everything is still.

But the sky ripples—subtle, faint, like a bruise spreading across reality.

A thin crack of Golden light tears through the stars, gone as quickly as it appears.

Evelyn shivers. "What was that?"

Adam doesn't answer immediately.

He knows this war is only pausing—not ending.

Nyarlathotep is wounded, not dead.

Dimensions are unstable.

And something vast still stirs beneath the fabric of the multiverse.

He thinks of Dex.

Of Jose.

Of Victor—another version of himself, broken in ways Adam only barely understands.

He squeezes Evelyn's hand gently.

"It's not over," he says. "But whatever comes next... we face it together."

Evelyn leans into him.

"Together," she echoes.

The auroras shimmer brighter, painting the ice in impossible colors.

Adam closes his eyes, breath steady, heart full.

For the first time since the war began—

He feels hope.

Real hope.

And far above the Antarctic sky, in the unseen corners of existence, something ancient shifts...

...watching.

Waiting.

The future is coming.

But Adam Warn—Ronin of Raptor Squad, survivor of gods and war—is ready.

About the author

Joseph Melugin Is a Man from Woodbridge, Virginia. This is his first work as an Author,

with his major interests is surrounding SCI-FI, Video Games, and Movies.

this book was a story he had since childhood and overtime evolved to what we read now as TURBO-TIME TROOPERS!

Also by

www.ingramcontent.com/pod-product-compliance
Lightning Source LLC
Chambersburg PA
CBHW051839170626
46807CB00003B/1260